FIRST CRUSH

FIRST CRUSH

MICHAEL HARTWIG

Contents

1

Chapter One – A Match

Patrick took a moment to contemplate the magnificent setting of his home high on the mountainous terrain overlooking the Amalfi Coast. He stood on the front porch of the cottage with a steaming cup of coffee in his hand. He peered out over the family vineyard toward the sea that shimmered in the distance. Bright yellow and green grape leaves, still wet from the morning dew, sparkled in the sunlight rising higher in the blue sky. Zeno, Patrick's husband, had taken Massimo, their son, to Zeno's parents. They would babysit while Zeno worked at the restaurant in Positano.

Patrick strolled around the corner of the house to examine the vegetable and herb garden. The first batch of tomatoes was just beginning to turn red. Patrick rubbed his hand on the large rosemary bush and lifted his fingers to his nose to inhale the pleasant fragrance. The basil plants were increasing in size, as were yellow squash, peppers, and a variety of greens. The branches of several lemon trees hung heavy with ripening fruit.

Patrick heard a sound nearby and noticed Pepe, his second cousin and the foreman of the estate, arranging tools he would use to trim the vines. Pepe looked up and waved to Patrick. Patrick nodded and walked down the gravel road toward Pepe's house.

"*Ciao, bello! Che fai?* What are you up to?" Patrick asked.

"Patrizio! What a pleasant surprise. I thought you had to work today," Pepe said in reply, giving Patrick an enthusiastic embrace and kisses on both cheeks.

"Later. I'm free this morning."

"Do you have a moment? I want to show you something."

Patrick nodded and followed Pepe into his house. He took a deep breath as he entered the calming space – a historic farmhouse that Pepe had decorated tastefully with Persian carpets, antiques, art, and comfortable chairs and sofa. As he pivoted in the living room, he asked, "Is that a new painting?"

"Do you like it? I just finished it."

"It's amazing. The sky and sea seem to blend in the horizon, and the boat has an ethereal look with its wispy sail."

Pepe blushed. "Thanks. Come in. Can I offer you some coffee or water?"

"Water would be nice. What did you want to show me?"

Pepe handed Patrick a glass of water and led him to the dining table, where he opened his laptop and typed in his password. "I think I found a match."

Patrick ran his hand over Pepe's muscular shoulder and said, "That's fantastic. Who is he?"

"Come look," Pepe said, pulling a chair up next to him and inviting Patrick to sit. Pepe clicked on the link, and a photograph of a handsome man appeared on the screen.

"*Bello!*" Patrick said, sighing.

"I thought he was handsome, too. But in a subtle way."

"What do you mean?"

"You know. He's not like the guys who post provocative photos or leave little to the imagination."

"Hmm. He's more serious, strait-laced, then?"

"Seemingly. We have common interests in literature and art."

"Sounds promising," Patrick said with a bit of regret. He and Zeno still had lingering affections for Pepe, and they continued to hope he might reconsider their brief experiment in the States. "And where does he live?"

"Sorrento."

"Local, then."

Pepe smiled and gazed at the photo. "We're making plans to meet up next week."

"Anyone else?"

Pepe sighed. "Not really. There are all sorts of guys ready to hook up. I never realized how easy it would be for a quick *scopata*."

Before Pepe came out, Patrick fully imagined he would be the kind of guy who would have engaged in all sorts of casual, anonymous sex. Pepe was amazingly sexy – with a seductive smile, luscious nose, playful dark hair, and an imposing physique – muscular pecs, thick biceps, and legs that strained the fabric of his shorts. Men and women found him irresistible. A year ago, Pepe courted women. But after a series of failed relationships, and a trip to Florida with Zeno and Patrick, he finally embraced his latent attraction to men.

During the trip to the States, Zeno, Patrick, and Pepe experimented with the idea of becoming a throuple. They had always been close, so the relationship side was easy. The sex was amazing. But the connection with Zeno and Patrick stirred Pepe's deep psychological discomfort at being an orphan, at being welcomed into a family but never quite having the same status as others. He decided he had to forge his own way and find a companion and husband for himself.

Zeno and Patrick helped him create a compelling profile – one that showcased Pepe's assets. There were clearly the physical ones, and Pepe's photograph generated a lot of interest. But Pepe wanted to find someone who was thoughtful – who liked to read, who appreciated art, and who valued family, traditions, and life in the countryside.

Giorgio was one of the first prospects to check all the boxes. He had classic southern Italian features – luminous caramel skin, dark wavy hair, and expressive brown eyes. He noted that he liked sports and worked out. Most importantly, for Pepe, he indicated he liked going to museums, attending lectures, reading novels, cooking, and travel.

"Is he going to come here?"

"No. I'm meeting him in Sorrento. He works at a hotel. We'll have dinner at a local restaurant."

"That sounds serious. Not just a drink?"

"We've been corresponding. I feel like I know him already."

As Pepe enumerated their common interests, Patrick sensed Pepe's enthusiasm, and he didn't want to dampen it. But he knew it was easy for two guys to tell each other what they thought the other wanted to hear. The truth would come out in the end, and he hoped Pepe wouldn't be disappointed.

"So, what do you think?"

Patrick raised a brow playfully, expressively. "He seems perfect for you. But be careful."

"I will."

"What are your plans for the day?"

"I have to do some trimming of the vines. You want to help?"

"Me? You know how I love manual labor."

"It's good for you."

"Maybe I could help for a bit. But I have to be at Nunzia's inn by two o'clock."

"We can work a bit, have lunch, and send you on your way."

"Let me change. I'll meet you in the field," Patrick said.

Pepe nodded excitedly.

Patrick retreated to his cottage, changed into work shorts and a tee shirt, and met Pepe in the vineyard. Pepe handed him some clippers, and they both began cutting the errant branches of the venerable vines.

"How are Zeno and Massimo?" Pepe began as he extended his arm to trim a few stems.

"They're good. Massimo is five going on ten. He seems so grown up and intelligent."

"He's surrounded by lots of adults."

"Hmm," Patrick murmured. "You're right. He doesn't have a lot of kids to play with."

"Are there any kindergartens he could join here in Italy?

"We're looking."

"And Zeno?"

"He's busy at the restaurant. He won't have a break until September."

"Ah, yes. The tourist season. And you? You must be busy at Nunzia's."

"Indeed. She's booked solid for the rest of the summer. This is the time of the year when there are lots of Brits and Germans. So, she relies on me a lot. The Italians come in July and August."

"Americans?"

"They haven't discovered Praiano. That's a good thing."

The air grew warm. Pepe perspired, and his cotton tee shirt became increasingly translucent. Patrick kept his cravings for Pepe in check, but there were times when the lure of his body was overwhelming. He glanced over and felt his legs grow weak and his self-restraint weaken.

Pepe looked up and smiled. He adored Patrick and sometimes wondered if he had made a big mistake not pursuing him six years ago. And while he knew he had to forge his own way, he missed the affection he and Patrick and Zeno shared while they were in the States. Patrick was handsome. He had Italian and Irish features – glowing skin that tanned in the Italian sun, playful thick hair, a broad forehead, and the Benevento nose. He was in good shape and had round, firm buttocks. His own cock quivered as he recalled their sexual adventures earlier in Florida and Boston.

The two of them continued to work the field and chat. Around noon, Pepe said, "Are you ready for a bit of lunch? I have some chicken and salad at home."

"I thought you'd never ask. I'm exhausted."

"Meet you at the house?" Pepe suggested.

Patrick nodded. He walked back to his cottage, stripped, showered, and put on some fresh clothes. He strolled to Pepe's house and walked inside.

Pepe had rinsed himself outside. He wore only a pair of shorts and flip-flops. The fragrance of the verbena soap Pepe used lingered in the air, and Patrick felt himself stir as he watched Pepe prepare lunch without a shirt on. "What can I do to help?"

"Can you open some wine?"

"Sure," Patrick said, opening a drawer, pulling out a corkscrew, and opening a bottle of the family *vino*.

Pepe tossed some salad with morsels of grilled chicken. They sat at the kitchen table, raised their glasses, and said, "*Salute*."

Between bites, Pepe leaned back in his chair, his chest and abdomen flexed provocatively at Patrick.

"Could you tone that down a bit?" Patrick insisted.

"*Scusa*," Pepe said apologetically, reaching for a pullover on a nearby chair.

"You don't have to put on a shirt. Just be less of a tease."

Pepe blushed. Then he said, "Just practicing."

"I thought you were looking for someone serious. You're not going to do that with Giorgio, are you?"

"They still have to be sexy."

"Zeno and I get the right of first refusal."

"What does that mean? I need your stamp of approval?"

"You need that, too. But first refusal means we have an option on the guy before you do."

Pepe lobbed a piece of salad at Patrick and said, "*Ma vaffanculo*."

"*Scerzo*. I'm kidding. But you know he will be under close scrutiny."

"You didn't seem that curious about my girlfriends."

Patrick grinned and looked off evasively. He turned back to Pepe and said, "They were doomed from the start."

Pepe cleared his throat for a response. He then swallowed and decided to keep silent. He realized Patrick was right. He realized that he had always been gay, or at least leaned in that direction. He had finally made peace with his inclinations, and it felt good.

They finished their lunches. Patrick stood and took his plate to the sink. As he passed behind Pepe, he ran his hand over Pepe's muscular shoulder. Pepe felt goosebumps run across his back, and he took hold of Patrick's hand. "I'm nervous."

"You'll be fine."

"I don't want to fuck up a good match."

"If it's a good match, you won't."

Pepe stood and faced Patrick. He wanted to kiss him. Patrick could feel the intensity in Pepe's eyes and the firming up of his own sex as he contemplated what he would like Pepe to do to him. He took a deep breath, continued to the sink, and washed his plate.

"Well, I need to get ready for work."

"Thanks for your help and support."

"Anytime. I'm sure we'll see you around."

They embraced. As Patrick left and walked home, Pepe retired to the living room, where he collapsed on the sofa and placed his hands over his face. "*Sono fottuto.* I'm fucked," he exclaimed, realizing how he pined for Patrick. He hoped Giorgio or someone like him might help him move on.

Patrick dressed and drove to Nunzia's inn. As he walked into the front parlor, Nunzia greeted him. "*Ciao, Patrizio!* I'm so glad you are here. We have a lot of high maintenance couples this week, and I need your diplomatic skills."

"At your service, my dear!"

Nunzia grinned. She ran a tight ship, and she didn't ordinarily let problematic guests get under her skin. She was effusive and warm, but knew how to maintain boundaries and keep people in check.

"See that couple over there?"

Patrick nodded.

"The woman is a princess. Thinks everything revolves around her. Her husband is more *simpatico* and rolls his eyes from time to time, as if he knows she's a pain. I've lost my patience. Maybe you can charm her."

"I'll try." Patrick took a deep breath and walked toward the couple. They were reclining on chaises and sipping mineral water. As Patrick approached, the man took off his sunglasses and looked up.

"*Sono Patrizio.* I work here with Nunzia."

"*Alessandro. Piacere,*" the man said, introducing himself. "And this is Giada."

"*Piacere.* Can I get you anything?"

Giada leaned up and glanced at Patrick. She gave him a frightful look. "Do you have any fresh towels? These have an odor to them." She scrunched her nose as she held up the edge of the towel she was sitting on.

Patrick glanced at Alessandro, who held his breath and rolled his eyes slightly upward as if to convey, as discreetly as possible, his apologies for her demand.

"*Subito.* Right away," Patrick said, retreating to the main building of the inn in search of fresh beach towels.

Inside, he gave Nunzia a playful look. "I see what you mean."

"Do whatever you can to appease her. She's connected to an important family in Milan, and I would hate for them to post bad reviews."

Patrick returned to Alessandro and Giada and handed them new towels. "Can I get you anything else?"

"Some more mineral water. Preferably with ice and lime," Giada said, without saying please or thank you.

Patrick peered at Alessandro and asked, "Anything for you?"

Alessandro paused. His eyes made a quick inventory of Patrick's assets - his muscular legs, slim waist, broad chest, and expressive eyes. The breeze whipped a few tufts of Patrick's playful hair over his broad forehead. He said, "No. I'm all set." Alessandro's response was measured, and it was clear he wanted to convey that he wasn't certain he was all set. He was curious what other services might be on the menu.

Patrick had been around enough to know Alessandro was scrutinizing him. And he imagined that if he had been married to Giada, he would be looking around for extracurricular activities, too. He sympathized with the man's dilemma, but knew it was best to be professional and maintain warm but firm boundaries. He had learned a lot from Nunzia.

Patrick excused himself and walked toward the edge of the lower terrace, where the turquoise blue water rocked several colorful wooden fishing boats moored to buoys. A couple of guests treaded water. Patrick collected empty glasses and plates and returned to the inn.

"Nunzia, besides keeping the guests happy, what else do you need today?"

"Franco needs help in the kitchen for dinner. Dario is sick."

"No problem. Anything else?"

"I'll review reservations and respond to emails. If you can keep an eye on the terrace, we should be good. I'm so glad you are here to help."

"It's my pleasure."

Patrick went into the kitchen where Franco was prepping things for dinner. Franco had worked with Nunzia for years. He was a local man who knew how to turn simple ingredients into exceptional dishes. The guests' favorites were grilled Seabass with green sauce, homemade pasta with pesto, caprese salad with local buffalo mozzarella, and grilled vegetables. "Franco. How are you?"

"Stressed. Dario is not coming in."

"What can I do to help?"

"Can you cut up the vegetables?"

Patrick nodded.

"And when you are finished, perhaps make the caprese salad?"

"How many guests for dinner tonight?"

"I think thirty or so."

"What's the main course?"

"Scallopine with a lemon and caper sauce."

"Hmm. One of my favorites!"

Patrick took out a large cutting board and used several restaurant-scale tools to slice vegetables. He oiled and seasoned them.

He looked out of the window and noticed Alessandro walking across the terrace. He was a tall, northern-Italian man with straw-colored skin that had, surprisingly, tanned well. He stood erect, with broad shoulders and a large head covered in tufted, dirty blonde hair. The black Speedo he wore hung loosely on his thin hips but clung tightly to his full, round buttocks. Patrick peered at the bulge in his crotch and murmured, "Hmm. Nice package."

Alessandro reached for a glass on the table next to his chaise and then pivoted, walking toward the kitchen. Patrick blushed and quickly focused on cutting peppers.

"*Con permesso.* Might I get more mineral water?" Alessandro asked Patrick as he stuck his head inside the door.

"*Certo,*" Patrick replied, reaching into the refrigerator, pulling out a bottle of water, and pouring Alessandro a glass.

Alessandro gave Patrick an intense look. Patrick felt his heart skip a beat. Alessandro's hazel eyes sparkled as he smiled warmly. He raised a brow playfully as Patrick finished filling the glass. "*Grazie,*" he said.

"*Prego.* Anything else?"

Alessandro nodded no. But his eyes suggested otherwise. Despite his blonde hair, his lashes were dark and wispy. The sunlight caught the distinguished contours of his temples that creased as he smiled. He walked back toward the deck, and Patrick couldn't help staring at the luscious profile of his body.

Franco had watched the entire exchange and said playfully, "I'm watching you."

"It's my job to get to know the guests and make sure they have what they need."

"Unless you and Zeno have a new arrangement, I'm not sure you can satisfy mister Milano there!"

"Franco. I'm offended by your implications."

"I just tell it as I see it!"

"Let's get back to work," Patrick said with a furrowed brow.

Later that evening, Patrick helped Nunzia serve guests. It was a busy evening, and Patrick ran back and forth between the kitchen and tables. He paid close attention to Giada and Alessandro, hoping they would be impressed by the food and service.

Giada didn't eat much. She was distracted by incoming messages on her phone. Alessandro was bored and drank copious amounts of white wine. Each time Patrick came to their table, Alessandro gazed into Patrick's eyes, hoping to solicit a wink or twinkle or some kind of acknowledgement of camaraderie.

Patrick sensed Alessandro's curiosity, but remained guarded. He had learned the hard way that friendly and flirty guests were a trap, and he didn't need trouble with them, Nunzia, or Zeno.

As dinner finished, Alessandro and Giada returned to their room. Patrick helped Franco and Nunzia clean up, and he returned to Cava dei Lupi, where Zeno was already in bed. He stripped and slid under the covers, pulling himself close to Zeno's warm body. He reached his arm over his side and squeezed him tightly. "*Buonanotte, tesoro!*" he whispered in Zeno's ear.

2

⟨❦⟩

Chapter Two – Giorgio

Pepe tried on several shirts before settling on a form-fitting, light blue pullover. He liked how it complemented his caramel tan skin and the dark shadow of a beard lining his jaw. It didn't hurt that the fabric clung to his impressive frame.

He held up a pair of jeans. "Hmm. These should do," he said as he stepped into the legs and pulled the fabric up to his waist. He glanced in the mirror and smiled contently at the nice cut of the garment. He slipped on a pair of light brown loafers and ran his hand through his thick, dark hair, peering closely at the reflection of himself, hoping everything was perfect.

He sighed, feeling both elated and anxious. His phone pinged. He leaned over and noticed a text from Giorgio. "Looking forward to meeting you in person. I'll see you at five, just outside of the hotel."

"*A presto,*" Pepe replied.

He slipped his billfold into his back pocket and walked outside, stepping inside his car. He turned on the ignition and sped down the road toward Praiano, where he picked up the curvy and picturesque roadway that ran along the Amalfi Coast. Without traffic, he would have arrived in Sorrento in about an hour, but it was tourist season, and the highway was crowded.

Pepe tried to enjoy the passing scenery – the rocky shoreline, small coves, and the deep blue Tyrrhenian Sea. But the ride was anything but relaxing given the wild drivers who defied reason and wove back and forth on the narrow pavement perched perilously high over the cascading terrain.

Eventually, he pulled into Sorrento with its enviable setting high above the Bay of Naples. The water glistened in the orange and purple hues of the sun peaking from behind distant clouds. He parked his car and walked a short distance to the hotel where Giorgio worked. He turned a corner and saw him leaning against a stone wall along a narrow street.

Giorgio was as handsome in person as he was in his profile photo. Pepe had been drawn to his affable smile, mysterious eyes, and dark, wavy hair. Giorgio sported a shortly cropped French mustache that circled his full, dark-red lips.

"Ciao," Giorgio said in a mellifluous voice, giving Pepe an embrace.

"Ciao," Pepe replied, rubbing Giorgio's shoulder and furtively examining his loose linen shirt and the contours of his chest underneath. "It's nice to meet you in person."

"Hmm. Yes," Giorgio replied. Giorgio's eyes widened as he scrutinized Pepe. He had been on many dates, but Pepe was by far the handsomest. He couldn't believe his luck. He took a deep breath and said, "I know a place nearby. We can get an apéro if you would like."

"Perfect."

As they walked toward the bar, both struggled to start a conversation, asking trivial questions.

"Your ride in? All good?"

"*Bene*," Pepe replied without elaboration. Nervously, he asked, "Is this where you work?"

"Yes. My uncle owns it."

Pepe imagined Giorgio dressed in a suit and greeting guests with charm and warmth at the front desk. "But your family is from Salerno, right?"

"Yes. But they live throughout Campania. Just like yours, I imagine."

Pepe blushed. He wasn't sure where his biological parents lived. He grew up in an orphanage in Salerno but lived as a teenager and young adult on the Benevento estate after Patrick's cousin, Alberto, adopted him. Pepe just nodded, preferring not to share too much about his origins. He asked a quick follow up question, "Did you work earlier today?"

"Yes. I took the morning shift. And you?"

"I make my own schedule."

Giorgio felt like they were off to an awkward start and was relieved when they arrived at the bar, where he looked forward to a stiff drink.

"Here we are," Giorgio said, putting his hand behind Pepe's back and leading him inside.

Pepe entered but wasn't prepared for the view in front of him. The bar opened onto a terrace that overlooked the entire Bay of Naples. The vista was breathtaking. "Oh, my God!" Pepe exclaimed.

"Yes. From the street, the place is unremarkable, and locals like to keep it a secret."

Giorgio nodded to one of the servers, and they took a seat on the edge of the balcony. Pepe looked down and tried to contain his anxiety. He didn't like heights.

"Too much?" Giorgio asked, noting Pepe's apprehension.

"Can we sit over there?" Pepe asked, spotting a table slightly inside.

Giorgio stood and took Pepe's hand. Pepe felt its warmth and detected Giorgio's gentleness as he led him to a table closer inside. Although it was a small gesture, Pepe was smitten by Giorgio's solicitous care.

They took seats, and Giorgio asked, "What would you like?"

Pepe wanted to say, 'you,' but decided to pace his enthusiasm. "Campari and soda."

Giorgio ordered drinks and then leaned over the small table and peered into Pepe's eyes. "Finally, we meet."

"I've enjoyed corresponding over the past couple of weeks," Pepe said in return. He had spent considerable effort convincing Giorgio that he was looking for more than a hook up. And while that was still his objective, he began to reconsider his priorities. There was something magnetic about Giorgio — the intensity of his eyes, the glow of his skin, the playfulness of his dark hair, and the heat that radiated from his hands resting just inches from Pepe's. Pepe began to undress Giorgio with his eyes, imagining what he might find when he unzipped his jeans and reached in to take hold of his cock.

"I have to say, your profile is unusual," Giorgio remarked, catching Pepe off-guard.

Pepe blushed.

Giorgio continued. "You're sexy and handsome, but there are so many fascinating layers to you. Your interest in art, literature, and history drew me in."

Pepe found Giorgio's remarks terribly arousing. His cock quivered thinking about having sex with a man who was both handsome and shared his cultural interests.

"I have to say the same. I can't believe you like to browse bookstores like me."

Giorgio looked away evasively. While he did share Pepe's interests, his visits to bookstores were more for cruising than literary purposes.

The server brought their drinks, and both raised their glasses and said, "*Salute!*"

"Do you have other family here in Sorrento?" Pepe asked.

"Just aunts and uncles?"

"Siblings?"

"A brother in Salerno," he replied, taking a sip of his drink. "And you?"

"Younger brother and sister on the vineyard," Pepe answered, concealing the fact that Gabi and Ricardo were not his biological siblings.

"So, you tend vines?"

Pepe fidgeted nervously with his napkin. He said timidly, "I'm kind of in charge of the whole operation – the vineyard itself and the production, aging, and bottling."

"Wow!"

Pepe nodded. "My father is in charge of marketing and sales."

"The name of the vineyard is Benevento. That's your name, right? Has it been in the family for a while?"

"Generations."

"That's amazing. I can't wait to visit."

"And you?"

"And me, what?"

"Hospitality? Hotel management?"

Almost imperceptibly, Giorgio twitched. He answered, "Everyone in the family shares in the work. We have several properties. I like the interaction with guests."

"I could see that. You seem personable. It must take a lot of patience."

"Yes. For the most part, people are nice."

"But there must be some guests who push the limits."

"Indeed," Giorgio said, raising a brow.

"Do any try to come onto you?"

Giorgio blushed. He sensed Pepe was testing the waters. "They do, but I remain professional."

Pepe sighed in relief. Giorgio was handsome and undoubtedly elicited interest from hotel guests. "You must get it from both sides – male and female."

Giorgio nodded. "The women are more persistent."

"But the men more difficult to dissuade?" Pepe asked, still trying to get a sense of Giorgio's moral compass.

"No. I can handle both sides."

Pepe's eyes widened, now intrigued. He wondered if Giorgio had just dropped a clue about being bisexual? He went right for the jugular. "Any girlfriends?"

"You mean me, now?"

"Now or in the past?"

"None now. A few failed ones in the past. And you?"

Pepe fidgeted in his chair. "The same. Nothing endured. Now I know why."

"Are you just coming out?"

Pepe didn't want to seem naïve or a neophyte. "No."

"Boyfriends, then?"

Pepe wasn't sure how to answer. Evasively he said, "Nothing that lasted."

"You?"

Giorgio wrung his hands and looked away from the table. He then turned to Pepe and said, "I'm wanting something more long-term. There are so many guys out there who just want to hook up. That's why I was drawn to your profile."

Pepe smiled contently. Giorgio was saying all the right things.

Giorgio finished his drink in one long gulp. "Should we head to dinner?"

Pepe nodded. Giorgio paid, and they walked outside. "There's a nice trattoria down the street."

Pepe followed Giorgio. They walked inside a small but classy establishment. The maître d' recognized Giorgio and gave them a nice table.

"More family?" Pepe asked in a low voice.

"No. But there's a lot of collaboration between the restaurant and the hotel."

"What do you suggest?"

"Everything is delicious. Seafood is their specialty — all freshly caught."

Pepe gave a quick glance at the menu, but couldn't take his eyes off of Giorgio. He breathed in the subtle scent of his cologne and studied his posture and gestures — classy and graceful. Giorgio folded his menu and set it on the table, staring into Pepe's dark eyes.

"What are you having?" Pepe asked.

"You mean, besides you?" Giorgio replied without blinking.

Pepe blushed. He hoped he was on the menu, but wasn't prepared for Giorgio's forwardness. Pepe raised a brow and nodded.

Giorgio continued, "I'm going to have the Branzino."

"I was thinking the same, but I love scampi and risotto."

Giorgio nodded to the waiter, who came to the table and took their orders. When he retreated to the kitchen, Giorgio leaned forward and said, "So, where were we?"

"Family?"

"Ah, yes. My family. We are all over the place."

"Are you out to them?" Pepe inquired.

Giorgio looked across the room, avoiding Pepe's eyes. He rubbed his hands together nervously. "Yes, and no."

"Sounds complicated."

"It is. My parents are fine, but my aunts and uncles, the ones who own the hotels, are not. They have a conservative and loyal clientele. I have to be discreet."

"What does that mean?"

"I just have to be careful."

"I get that."

"And you?"

"My family knows."

"And are they okay?"

Pepe nodded. "Yes. Although it's still rather new to them."

"Are you just coming out?"

Pepe pondered his response. In retrospect, he realized he had been gay for quite some time. Even though he had not embraced his identity or declared it until recently, his orientation was not new, and his family had long suspected – at least Alberto, Patrick, and Zeno had. "No. I've known for a while."

The waiter came with their appetizers. Pepe raised his glass of wine and said, "*Buon appetito.*"

Giorgio nodded. They both began to eat.

Pepe glanced up at Giorgio. He wondered why he was still available. Why hadn't he been snatched up? He was handsome, affable, and employed. He wondered if, like him, he was discriminating, looking for a partner. Maybe he could be that for Giorgio.

Giorgio sensed Pepe's curiosity and looked up over his plate. Their eyes connected, and each smiled contently. Pepe sighed.

"You said in one of your emails that you like to read," Giorgio said.

"Since I was a teenager. I was lucky to have access to good books."

"On the vineyard?"

"Yes. One wouldn't suspect."

"Is your father a literary person?"

"No. But my predecessor was?"

"Predecessor?"

Pepe realized he had slipped up and exposed an inconsistency in his story. "I mean, one of my ancestors. Since I was older, I have lived in a separate building on the estate. One of my great uncles lived there, and he was a philosopher, artist, and reader."

"Just like you!"

"Yes. It would seem."

"Do you paint, too?"

Pepe nodded.

"I would like to see what you've done."

"That can be arranged. And you? You seem very interested in history and archaeology."

"If you grow up in Campania, you have to develop some kind of appreciation for the heritage of the area. There are too many exceptional archaeological sites not to."

Pepe nodded, realizing that between Herculaneum, Pompeii, Paestum and countless other smaller excavations, the region was rich in historical layers. "I'm a fan of the Farnese collection at the archaeological museum in Naples," Pepe offered.

"Me too," Giorgio said with a big grin. "There's a new exhibition there. Maybe we can go together."

"That would be nice."

They continued to chat, eat, and explore common interests. Neither had agreed to anything other than dinner. Pepe hadn't wanted to commit to something without meeting Giorgio first. Throughout the course of their dinner, Pepe grew more comfortable with Giorgio's personality — his traditional values, curiosity, and charm. When he first posted a profile with Patrick's and Zeno's help, Pepe protested to them that sexual chemistry, which he considered crucial to a relationship, was difficult to determine over the internet. Giorgio was clearly handsome, but something else took hold of Pepe as they spent time together.

As Giorgio finished the last morsels of his Branzino, he glanced at his watch. Pepe feared he was contemplating an exit. Instead, Giorgio said, "I don't know how eager you are to get back home, but if you are up for it, we could go back to my place for a drink."

Pepe could hardly contain himself. He grinned contently and nodded. "That would be nice."

Giorgio waved down the waiter, settled the bill, and led Pepe outdoors. They walked a few blocks to a historic apartment building. Giorgio led Pepe upstairs and unlocked the door. "Here's my humble home."

Just inside the door, Pepe pivoted toward Giorgio, took hold of his head, and pulled him close, giving him an enthusiastic kiss. Giorgio took a deep breath, and kissed Pepe back, running his hands along Pepe's back and squeezing his firm, round buttocks.

Giorgio closed the door behind him, and Pepe quickly began to unbutton Giorgio's shirt, sliding his hands inside the fabric and running them over Giorgio's lean chest. Giorgio pushed Pepe toward the center of the room and pressed him down on the sofa. He straddled him and ran his hand up under Pepe's pullover, feeling his firm, muscular pecs underneath. "*Quanto sei bello!*" Giorgio murmured in Pepe's ear, running his wet lips down Pepe's neck.

For a brief moment, Pepe became apprehensive. Certain things could trigger painful memories of past abuse, and being cornered, particularly by someone he just met, was a problem. He slid out from under Giorgio, who leaned back and unzipped his own jeans. They were both eager to consume the desire that had been building all evening.

Pepe raised his brows when Giorgio pulled out his thick, dark cock. Instinctively, Pepe leaned forward and took Giorgio in his mouth. Giorgio moaned as Pepe's warm, wet lips encircled him. Pepe was now in charge, and he wanted to devour his partner.

Pepe pressed Giorgio down on the cushions of the sofa. He unzipped his own jeans and slid them down his muscular thighs. Giorgio ran his hand over the hardness pressing against Pepe's undershorts. He yanked the shorts down and took hold of Pepe's erection, shimmering in the ambient lighting of the room.

Both paused briefly, uncertain of each other's preferences. Each was grateful as their bodies took over, speaking a language of their own. Pepe pulled a condom out of his jeans and slipped it on his firm sex. He leaned back over Giorgio, spit in his hand, and ran his fingers along the inside of his crack. As Pepe slid himself into Giorgio and took possession of him, Giorgio murmured in delight. He gave himself over to the solidity of Pepe's body as it invaded his own. Pepe peered down at the man under him – classy, sophisticated, handsome. His eyes were dark and mysterious, his smile warm and welcoming, and his skin smooth and hot.

Pepe took Giorgio's cock in his hand and began to run his fingers up and down its length. Giorgio's back arched as he felt waves of intense pleasure coursed up his legs.

Giorgio leaned forward and ran his hand over Pepe's chest, now wet with perspiration. Pepe's pecs hardened as he became increasingly aroused, and Giorgio could hardly contain his excitement. He felt his body travel to another dimension, relinquishing all bound-aries as Pepe filled him and held him.

Suddenly, he felt Pepe come inside him in a series of powerful bursts. He, in turn, exploded in Pepe's hand. Pepe collapsed on top of him. As the final tremors of their exchange subsided, Giorgio ran his hand over Pepe's back and said, "Wow! You're amazing!"

"Hmm," Pepe murmured.

Giorgio extracted himself from Pepe, reached for his shorts, and walked across the room toward the kitchen. Pepe leaned up and slipped on his shorts.

"You ready for that drink?" Giorgio asked with a wink.

Pepe chuckled and nodded.

Giorgio poured them both a glass of brandy, and they sat qui-etly on the sofa.

"This was nice," Giorgio said, breaking the awkward silence.

"Yes. I agree."

Both took a long sip of their drinks. Giorgio added, "Do you want to stay over?"

Pepe didn't answer at first. He gazed into the amber liquid in his glass and swirled it around. "Thanks for the offer, but I have work early tomorrow."

"I'd like to see you again," Giorgio added.

"Me, too."

"What are you doing later in the week? Would you like to go to the exhibit at the archaeological museum in Naples?"

"That would be nice. I could pick you up, and we could drive there together."

Giorgio nodded, but looked deep in thought. He pleaded, "Stay."

"I can't. I have to go." Pepe finished his drink in one last gulp and put on his clothes.

Giorgio approached him and gave him a warm embrace and then kissed him. "I'll call."

"That would be nice."

Pepe walked toward the door, and Giorgio held his hand. They kissed again, and Pepe walked down the stairs and out onto the street, retracing his steps toward his car. He drove home along the coastal route.

The next morning, Pepe knocked on Patrick's and Zeno's door and let himself in. Patrick was pouring milk into Massimo's bowl of cereal, and Zeno was making espresso.

"Pepe!" Zeno said enthusiastically as he saw him walk in. "Tell us all about it!"

"Can you make me an espresso first?" Pepe replied, trying to contain his excitement.

Zeno nodded and prepared the coffee. Patrick retrieved Massimo's tablet and set it next to him. He grabbed a croissant and invited Pepe and Zeno outside to the front porch, where the adults could have a conversation.

"Well?" Patrick inquired.

Pepe sighed. "It was perfect."

Zeno gave Pepe an encouraging look, and Pepe continued. "He's very nice. Handsome. Thoughtful. Curious. Interesting."

"And?" Zeno pressed. "Get to the good part."

"That was the good part," Pepe said, grinning.

Patrick and Zeno furrowed their brows.

Pepe said, "Oh. That."

"Yes," Patrick interjected. "That."

"Well, we hadn't planned anything. You know me and chemistry. I need to sense something, get a feel for someone in person."

"And?" Zeno said, taking a sip of his coffee.

"Conversation at dinner was easy. There wasn't anything off-putting – no strange mannerisms, smells, gestures, red flags. I could feel myself being drawn in, and I think it was reciprocal. He invited me to his place for a drink, and well, you know."

Zeno and Patrick glanced at each other and said, "Details!"

Pepe blushed. Patrick noticed and said, "You don't have to tell us anything. We're glad to hear things went well. Do you have another date planned?"

"Day after tomorrow. We are going to the archaeological museum in Naples."

"So, he's a geek?" Patrick asked.

Pepe shook his head. He didn't know what the term 'geek' meant.

"An intellectual. You know, boring," Patrick added.

"He likes cultural things, but he's not snooty."

"How do you think he will do here, on the vineyard?"

"He's from the area. He must have relatives who have property. I'm sure he's fine with it," Pepe said hesitatingly.

"We're happy for you," Zeno noted, sensing Pepe's discomfort with their interrogation. "Just be careful."

"I will. He seems very nice."

"What's on the agenda today?" Patrick inquired.

"I have some work up at the cellar with Alberto. And you guys?"

"I'm off. Although Zeno has to work this evening, so I will be taking care of Massimo."

"Do you and Massimo want to help at the cellar this afternoon?"

"Sure. We'll meet you there later."

"Okay, guys. I have to go."

"Don't text him too often," Zeno advised. "You don't want him to think you are desperate or clingy."

Pepe blushed. He had already texted Giorgio earlier.

3

Chapter Three – The Farnese Collection

Two days later, Pepe pulled up in front of Giorgio's family hotel in Sorrento. Giorgio waved and got into the car. They sped off towards Naples.

"*Ciao, bello!*" Giorgio said, running his hand along Pepe's leg.

"*Ciao,*" Pepe said, sighing. He breathed in Giorgio's scent and grazed his hand as he shifted gears. He could hardly contain himself.

Pepe sped along the curvy road and picked up the highway leading into Naples. "You have the tickets?" Giorgio inquired.

Pepe nodded. "And I made reservations for lunch later. A cool place in the old city."

"How is work?"

"Not too bad this time of the year. And you?"

"The calm before the storm. July and August are crazy. When was the last time you went to the archaeological museum?" Giorgio asked.

"Several years ago. And you?"

"The same. I always seem to see or notice something new."

"Do you have a favorite in the museum? Pepe asked.

"The Farnese Bull."

"Because?" Pepe pressed.

"I don't know. Perhaps because of its size, its composition, and the history of its discovery."

"Can you imagine archaeologists and artists in the 16th century as they explored Rome and found statues like that? I have always liked the Laocoön at the Vatican Museums, one that Michelangelo was present for when it was unearthed," Pepe said.

"Hmm. Yes, it's magnificent. And have you seen the monumental mosaics of the nude athletes there?"

"Yes. I believe they came from the same place as the Farnese Bull, the Baths of Caracalla."

"You know your history!" Giorgio remarked. "I'm impressed. Our vintner does more than make wine!"

Pepe felt his heart pound excitedly. He never imagined someone would appreciate or share his interests. That Giorgio was also handsome made their budding relationship even more promising. Pepe exited the highway and wove through the streets of Naples. They parked near the museum and joined the line for their timed entry.

Once inside, Giorgio took Pepe's elbow and led him into the Farnese section of the museum. The first part of the collection was impressive, but Pepe knew the monumental pieces were deeper in the exhibit hall. "I never remember how the collection ended up in Naples," Giorgio asked as they strolled past several pieces.

"My understanding is that as the Farnese family died out, the last heiress was Elizabeth, who married Philip V of Spain. Their son, Charles the Bourbon, became king of Naples and Sicily in the 18th century and took the collection with him."

"Before that, it was in the family palace in Rome, right?" Giorgio inquired.

Pepe nodded and gazed at the impressive male nudes. It was the first time visiting the museum after having come out, and he thought to himself how different it felt. Before he had strolled through the place by himself or with a girlfriend. Now, he was walking side by side, almost hand in hand, with a man every bit as handsome as the Roman and Greek gods. They were no longer mere curiosities of history. They embodied the virility and power of the male body, which he hoped to consume later in the day. He pondered the Renaissance artists and popes and realized how pervasive homoeroticism must have been amongst them. He grinned and gazed at the tilted head of Antinous, Hadrian's lover, glancing down seductively.

As they strolled into the grand hall, the breathtaking statue of Hercules came into view. Both stopped in their tracks and contemplated the larger-than-life muscular god leaning on his club. Giorgio circled the statue counterclockwise, and Pepe remained in place, moving ever so slowly in the other direction. At one point, Pepe lowered his gaze from the god's torso and noticed Giorgio on the other side of the sculpture, staring at Pepe. Their eyes connected, and Pepe felt his legs grow weak. Giorgio stood contrapposto; his light sweater draped over his shoulders. He looked so distinguished, classy, and dreamy. Pepe walked toward him and placed his hand on Giorgio's forearm. "It's magnificent, isn't it?"

Giorgio didn't miss the double entendre of Pepe's question. He peered intensely into Pepe's eyes and nodded.

They walked toward the end of the grand gallery to the Farnese Bull, the largest marble piece ever recovered from antiquity. It was a complicated carving, with Dirce being tied to a bull by Amphion and Zethus, two sons of Zeus. Their mother, Antiope, had been treated badly by Dirce, so the sons wanted to kill her.

"I'm always impressed by the intricacy of the work – the bodies so entwined and forceful," Giorgio noted.

Pepe nodded, his mouth wide open in amazement. "Look at how the artist has made the two men's capes seem like fabric blowing in the wind."

"And their pose!" Giorgio said expressively, referring to the way the artist had angled the front and back of the nude men so that their assets were clearly on display and a focus of attention.

"Hmm. Yes," Pepe murmured as he contemplated the scene.

Giorgio and Pepe stood mesmerized in front of the statue. Pepe grazed his hand against Giorgio's, just enough to let Giorgio know who was on his mind.

At one point, Giorgio turned to Pepe and smiled warmly. "Shall we?"

They continued their tour of the Farnese Collection and then strolled through the galleries filled with ancient Roman and Greek statues from the Campania region. As they finished visiting the ground floor, Giorgio asked, "Do you want to see the mosaics and frescos?"

"I could if you want to, but I'm also ready for lunch."

"Me, too. Let's go eat!"

They walked outside into the bright sunlight. Pepe said, "The restaurant I found is in this direction." He pointed down a side street and led Giorgio across a busy boulevard and into the historic center of the city. There had been a concerted effort in recent years to improve the look of the narrow streets and tall tenement buildings. Tourists had returned to the historical center of Naples, now filled with cafes, shops, and restaurants. Pepe took Giorgio's arm and pressed through one of the crowded streets. He made several turns and arrived at a small piazza, where umbrella covered tables spilled out of a restaurant onto cobblestone pavement. "Here it is," Pepe said proudly.

Giorgio nodded and followed Pepe inside. The maître d' showed them a nice table outside and brought them cool white wine.

"Ah, pasta Genovese," Giorgio noted as he studied the menu. "I still don't understand why it is so popular in Naples. We're a long way from Genoa."

"I understand it has to do with sailors who made their way from Genoa to Naples and other places along the coast."

"Well, it's one of my favorites," Giorgio said, setting the menu on the table and staring into Pepe's eyes.

Pepe grew nervous and took a long sip of his wine. Thankfully, the waiter returned and took their orders.

Giorgio lifted his glass to Pepe and said, "*Salute*. To more adventures in the future!"

"*Salute!*" Pepe replied.

"It's nice to find someone who has similar tastes and interests," Giorgio said, placing his hand near Pepe's.

"Yes. It is." Pepe smiled, but worrisome thoughts raced through his head. Would Giorgio warm up to the farm and to his work on the vineyard? And how would Pepe's family – including Patrick and Zeno – react to a boyfriend? Shifting focus, he asked, "Were your parents into the arts?"

"God, no," Giorgio said dramatically. "My father is a businessman, and my mother is rather simple. And you? Did your parents expose you to cultural things?"

Pepe froze. He looked off into the distance in search of a good answer. "My father paints, and as I told you, my great uncle had a lot of books. I guess I picked things up by osmosis."

"Where did you go to school?"

Pepe began to perspire. He didn't want to be dishonest, but he wasn't ready to share information about his childhood. It was too painful. He couldn't say Salerno, since Giorgio was from there. "A local school near Praiano."

"Ah. And did you grow up working on the estate?"

Pepe nodded and then tried to change the subject. "So, what kind of business is your father in?"

"He runs a group of small grocery stores."

"How did you escape that?" Pepe said with a grin.

"Why do you think I wanted to escape?"

Pepe leaned back and gave Giorgio a scrutinizing look. "I can't see you doing that. I can see you in hospitality, in a classy hotel, but not running back and forth between stores, making sure things are stocked and accounts in order."

It was now Giorgio's turn to give Pepe a look. He was more dramatic – tracing his hand dramatically over Pepe's torso. "And I can't see you as a farmer."

"Why not?"

"You have the build for it, most definitely!" Giorgio said, wetting his lips.

Pepe blushed.

"But I can't see that being enough for you."

Pepe felt a pinch in his chest. It was the same line his girlfriends had delivered before. He worried, now, that Giorgio wasn't, in fact, a good match. "First of all," Pepe began earnestly. "I'm not a farmer."

"But you work the land."

"I'm a vintner. I tend vines, old vines. It's an art and a science."

"Okay."

"And then I make wine. That, too, is an art and requires a lot of skill and intuition."

"*Scusa*. I'm sorry. I didn't mean to imply."

"It's okay. Most people don't understand."

"I'd like to visit the vineyard."

"That can be arranged," Pepe said, thinking carefully about how to introduce Giorgio to Patrick, Zeno, Alberto, and others.

The waiter approached their table with their lunches. Giorgio had ordered pasta Genovese, ziti covered in slow cooked onions and small pieces of beef. Pepe opted for a simple plate of spaghetti with tomatoes and basil. "*Buon appetito*," they both said to each other.

Pepe was relieved that there was a break in the conversation. Both ate their meals in relative silence. After finishing, they ordered espresso. Giorgio looked at his watch, and Pepe grew nervous that he was having second thoughts about them.

"Should we head back?" Pepe asked.

Giorgio glanced at his phone and noticed a text. He nodded. "It's been nice."

They paid their bill and walked to Pepe's car. He navigated the heavy traffic of the city and picked up the coastal road to Sorrento. Giorgio was quiet but affectionate, resting his hand on Pepe's thigh and sliding it occasionally toward Pepe's aroused cock pressing against the fabric of his jeans. Pepe did everything he could to contain himself, focusing on the road and asking banal questions of Giorgio.

Giorgio continued to glance at his phone as texts appeared. He seemed preoccupied and a bit unsettled. As they pulled into the center of town, Pepe hoped Giorgio might invite him to his apartment. They pulled up near the hotel, and there was an awkward silence. Giorgio said, "I would invite you to my place for a drink, but I have a cousin staying there."

Pepe was uncertain whether Giorgio really had a cousin at his apartment or if he was having second thoughts. "That's okay," Pepe said. "I have to get back to work, anyway."

"How urgent?" Giorgio interjected.

"I'm flexible. Why?"

"I know a secluded cove nearby. We could take a swim."

Pepe's eyes widened. He nodded.

"This way," Giorgio directed him.

Pepe followed Giorgio's directions. They made several turns in town and took a small winding road toward the water. "We have to walk down this path," Giorgio said as they parked the car at the edge of a vineyard.

They wandered down the hill to an inlet formed by several large boulders.

"This is beautiful," Pepe remarked, staring into the clear blue water.

Giorgio began to disrobe, and Pepe followed. Giorgio dove into the water and swam away from the shore. Pepe jumped in after him. He treaded up to Giorgio and gazed into his sparkling eyes. He leaned forward and gave him a kiss.

Giorgio reached his arms around Pepe and pulled him close, feeling Pepe's thick shaft under him. He gazed into Pepe's dark eyes and felt his heart pound forcefully. The lapping of the gentle waves tossed them about, and both clung tightly to one another.

Giorgio felt the tip of his cock quiver as it rubbed against Pepe's abdomen. Pepe, in turn, continued to press himself into the folds of Giorgio's buttocks bobbing over him.

Giorgio pivoted and swam out to deeper water, clearly hoping Pepe might follow. Pepe watched Giorgio's white, round buttocks glide across the surface of the turquoise blue water, and he crazily chased him, grabbing him from behind, holding his chest, and then sliding his cock up and down Giorgio's back side. Giorgio moaned with delight as Pepe seized him, held him, and consumed him.

It didn't take long for Pepe to come, as Giorgio twisted in the water. They treaded toward shallower water, and Pepe took hold of Giorgio's long, hard shaft and stroked it. Giorgio screamed as Pepe's warm hands slid up and down in the slippery, briny water. He let out a final moan as he came, and fell back in the buoyant water, gazing up at the sky.

"Wow!" Giorgio said, taking Pepe's hand and leading to the shore. They sat on the rocks and let the sun dry them. Pepe wondered how Giorgio knew of the place and how many guys he had led down the path to the secluded spot.

As much as he enjoyed their escapade and treasured Giorgio's cultural interests, he began to worry that something wasn't up.

"I love these secluded coves," Pepe inquired. "How did you discover this one?"

"My cousin brought me here one day. It's preferable to the busy bathing establishments run by hotels. For him, it was a break from all the tourists."

Pepe chuckled. "I have an aunt who runs an inn in Praiano. She has a nice swimming area that is exclusive to the hotel."

"That must be nice. What's the name of the place? I might know it."

"The Belvedere. It's a common hotel name."

Giorgio shook his head. He wasn't familiar with it. "Should we head back? I need to work later."

"Sure. This was fun," Pepe said as he reached for his shirt, undershorts, and shorts and slipped them on.

Giorgio approached Pepe and ran his hand through Pepe's hair, putting things back in place. "We need to make you presentable."

"I would suggest you put your clothes on then."

"Oh. Yes. I guess I should," he said, raising a brow. Gorgio dressed and led Pepe up the hill back to the car.

They drove back to Sorrento, where Pepe dropped Giorgio off at the hotel. Pepe drove to Cava dei Lupi, changed, and took care of some work. Before retiring for the evening, he texted Giorgio and thanked him for the afternoon.

4

Chapter Four – Change of Plans

A week later, Pepe rose early and made himself an espresso. He was eager for his third date with Giorgio. Giorgio had taken the day off, and they were going to visit the archaeological site at Cuma. Pepe had read about the Sibyl of Cumae, the rites associated with her oracle, and the famous Sibylline Books that ancient Roman senators consulted.

Pepe sat at the kitchen table and had some muesli, yogurt and fruit as he checked email. A text arrived from Giorgio.

"*Ciao, Pepe.* How are you doing? I have some bad news. There's an emergency at the hotel, and I have to work. Can we reschedule our excursion?"

Pepe sighed deeply and slumped over the table. "*Cazzo!*" he exclaimed. He texted back. "Too bad. I was looking forward to seeing you."

"I know. Me, too. I'll text when I know my schedule and we can set another date." Giorgio added a heart emoji in the text.

Pepe felt bad, but was encouraged when he saw the red heart on his phone screen. He cleaned up the kitchen, showered, and walked to the cellar to take care of some chores. As he entered the building, he realized there was a pending order for a restaurant not far from where Giorgio worked. He could make the delivery and then surprise Giorgio, stopping by to say hello.

Later, Pepe loaded a couple of cases of wine in his car and drove west. He made the delivery and then continued to the center of town, where he parked and walked to Giorgio's hotel. A handsome young man, Sandrino, greeted him at the front desk.

"*Buongiorno.* Is Giorgio here?" Pepe asked.

"I'm sorry," Sandrino replied, thinking quickly on his feet. "I had to send him on an errand. He won't be back for a while."

"Too bad. Can you let him know Pepe stopped by to say hello?"

Sandrino smiled and nodded. "Of course. He'll be sorry he missed you."

Pepe shook Sandrino's hand and walked out the door. He sped off toward the Benevento estate.

Meanwhile, Sandrino called Giorgio, who was really Rocco. Giorgio was just an alias Rocco used on dating apps and for hookups. In fact, Giorgio (really Rocco) didn't work at the hotel. That was a cover, too. He was a schoolteacher in Naples.

"*Pronto,*" Rocco answered as he saw the call come in from his cousin.

"Your boyfriend was just here," Sandrino said sternly.

"You're kidding."

"He's a handsome one!"

"Sandrino. Be serious. Was he really there?"

"Yes. He was looking for Giorgio. Are you still using that cover?"

"You know Ercole. He is always suspicious. I can't use my name."

"You need to be careful. This isn't going to turn out well."

"I don't know what to do."

"Talk to Ercole and tell him it's not working out between the two of you."

"Are you kidding? You know he has a terrible temper and will get violent. He thinks everything is fine as it is."

"Where are you?"

"I had made plans with Pepe, but then Ercole and his friends wanted to meet up in Positano for someone's birthday. I can't get out of it. I had to cancel on Pepe. He must have wanted to surprise me. It's cute."

"It's a disaster waiting to happen. Be honest with him and with Ercole."

"I'm working on it. Thanks for covering for me."

"I don't like it."

"You're a dear."

"You're a mess."

"*Ciao.*"

"*Ciao,*" Sandrino concluded and hung up.

Rocco hung up his phone and walked back to Ercole and his colleagues from the police force. "Who was that?" Ercole asked.

"Work."

"Why would the school be calling you on a Saturday?"

"Marta was following up on some documents we had to turn into the government."

"Everything good?"

"Yes," Rocco answered, although he was restless and unnerved. He decided he needed a drink. He walked through a row of chaises facing the sea. The scent of sunscreen floated in the warm, heavy air. Although there were a fair number of handsome men stretched out in the sun, Rocco was preoccupied and proceeded swiftly to the bar.

An unusually attractive waiter prepared drinks. He had alluring eyes, wispy lashes and thick brows. He glanced up as Rocco approached the bar and asked, "What can I get for you?"

"A gin and tonic," Rocco replied.

Zeno gave Rocco a second glance. He felt like he knew him from some place. He poured some gin in a glass and searched his memory for clues. Suddenly, he realized the guy was Giorgio, the man Pepe had identified on the dating app. Zeno smiled as he handed Rocco his drink and said, "Are you by any chance, Giorgio?"

Rocco felt dizzy and feared he might pass out. Could the bartender have been someone he slept with once, using the same alias? He nodded no. He was not Giorgio.

Ercole approached the bar and said, "*Tesoro*, dear, can you get me a glass of white wine?"

Zeno glanced back and forth at Ercole, who ran his hand over Rocco's shoulder - the man he thought was Giorgio. Another of Ercole's friends yelled from the chaises. "Rocco, can you get me a beer?"

Zeno poured Ercole a glass of white wine and opened a bottle of beer for the other friend. Rocco took care of the tab and returned to the gaggle of gay friends on the beach.

Zeno texted Patrick. "*Ciao, tesoro*. Do you have a photograph of Giorgio, Pepe's boyfriend?"

"Sure. Why?"

"I think he's here at the beach. But he claims his name is Rocco, not Giorgio.

Patrick texted Zeno a photograph, and Zeno held up his phone to compare the photograph and the man stretched out on the chaise. The man was definitely Pepe's boyfriend, whatever his name might be.

"I think we have a problem," Zeno texted Patrick. "Pepe's dating someone who seems to be involved with someone else. He looks like a cop, and his friends do, too."

"Shit!" Patrick texted back. "Should we tell Pepe?"

"Yes. I didn't have a good feeling about him from the start. Pepe needs to know he's being played."

Patrick hesitated, but realized Zeno was right. Better to get it out in the open quickly. "I'll text Pepe."

Patrick texted Pepe about the Giorgio sighting on the beach. Pepe was near Positano on his way back from Sorrento and decided to take a look himself. He parked in the restaurant parking lot and walked down the hill to the restaurant. He strolled to the bar area.

"*Salute*," he said to Zeno, glancing all the while at the beach.

Zeno leaned over the bar and gave him a kiss. "Patrick must have texted you."

"Um-hum. Where is he?"

Zeno pointed to the group of guys on the edge of the seating area on the sand. The big one is Ercole. I have a feeling he and Giorgio or Rocco or whoever he is are involved, perhaps as partners."

"What would you like to drink?"

"Water."

Zeno gave him a curious look and poured him a glass of mineral water.

Soon, Ercole walked toward the bar to order more drinks for his friends. He was a burly guy with dark, curly hair and a scruffy beard. He gave Pepe an intense look as he ordered drinks for his friends. Soon Rocco approached the bar and placed his hand on the small of Ercole's back. He looked across the bar and noticed Pepe. He turned beet red and froze in place.

Pepe gave him a stern look, and then his eyes began to turn red. A tear streaked down his cheek. He stood up and walked away.

Rocco didn't know what to do. He wanted to chase after Pepe, but Ercole was standing beside him. Rocco couldn't afford Ercole finding out about his indiscretions. Zeno handed Ercole the drinks he ordered and gave Rocco a punishing look. Ercole looked quizzically at Zeno, and then at Rocco. "Is there a problem?" he asked Zeno.

"Ask your friend," Zeno replied.

Ercole handed two of the drinks to Rocco, who said matter-of-factly, "There's no problem."

5

Chapter Five – Glances

Pepe got into his car and sped off angrily. He tailgated slow drivers, navigating the curvy and perilous road along the coast. Frustrated, he pulled into Nunzia's inn, where he knew Patrick was at work. He parked the car and walked briskly into the lobby.

"Pepe!" Nunzia said in surprise.

"Nunzia. How are you?"

"Better question. How are you?" she asked, noting his disheveled hair and the frightful look on his face.

"Fine. Where's Patrick?"

"On the terrace with some of the guests. Can I help you?"

"I need to speak with him." Pepe walked past Nunzia and out onto the deck.

Patrick looked up and excused himself from someone he was serving. He spotted Nunzia in the doorway, giving him a curious look.

Pepe paced frenetically on the deck with his fingers pressed against his forehead. "*Cazzo!*" he exclaimed loudly.

Patrick took him by the elbow, and they walked to the lower deck by the water. It was more private.

"You must have seen Giorgio, or whomever he calls himself."

Pepe nodded. "With a boyfriend or partner. Big burly guy."

"Hmm. Yes. Zeno texted me when he saw him. We're so sorry."

"I should have known. It was too perfect."

"You deserve perfect, but there are a lot of assholes out there who take advantage of people."

"He seemed different, genuine."

"Tell me what happened."

"We had a date, but he canceled. He said there was an emergency at work. I made a delivery in the Sorrento area and stopped by the hotel. They said they sent him on an errand. That's when I got your text that Zeno had spotted him on the beach."

"And what happened when you showed up?"

"He came to the bar to help his boyfriend, Ercole, with the drinks. He spotted me and froze."

"Then what happened?"

"I stood up and left."

Nunzia walked down toward them with a carafe of wine and a glass. "You probably need this," she said solicitously.

"*Grazie*," he said, filling a glass and taking a long sip.

"Make yourself at home. Take a swim. It does wonders."

Pepe nodded. Patrick smiled. Nunzia retreated to the upper deck.

Patrick noticed Alessandro sitting off to the side, observing them. When his and Patrick's eyes connected, he nodded.

Patrick pulled up a couple of chairs, and he and Pepe sat down. Pepe took another sip of wine. "Men are such pigs," he interjected.

"Not all of them."

"*Scusa*. Not you and Zeno."

"You'll find someone. You are just getting started. Giorgio or Rocco or whomever is an unfortunate lesson."

"I should have been suspicious when I didn't see his name on the hotel website or find him on any social media."

"You're off the radar, too."

"Hmm," Pepe moaned. He glanced over and noticed Alessandro staring at him.

"And who's that with the roving eye?"

"Alessandro. From Milan."

"Available?"

"Married."

"Could have fooled me."

"Has a princess for a wife. She's a pain. I detect he is restless, perhaps even for our team."

"Not bad looking," Pepe noted with a grin.

"That's the old Pepe I know," Patrick said, relieved that Pepe seemed to be moving on rather quickly, in fact.

Pepe blushed. He took a sip of wine to conceal a protracted scan of Alessandro's physique – his long legs, his broad shoulders, his dark blond tousled hair, and his enigmatic eyes. Alessandro rested a book on his crotch but didn't seem to be turning any pages.

"I have to go back. Alberto is waiting for me."

"We can talk tonight, if you like. I'll be home for dinner. Zeno will, too."

"I don't know if I'm up for socializing. We'll see."

"I'll walk you to your car," Patrick offered.

Pepe nodded. He stood and picked up the carafe and wine glass. He glanced toward the edge of the deck, where couples were reclining in the sun or dangling their feet in the water. They were, for the most part, an older crowd – except for Alessandro. He was alone and off to the side. He continued to peer in his and Patrick's direction, clearly intrigued. Pepe gave him one last glimpse as he followed Patrick. Their eyes connected, and Pepe felt a flutter in his stomach.

6

Chapter Six – A Month Later

A month later, Patrick drove to work. When he arrived in the hotel lobby, he saw Alessandro, who stood at the reception desk with his luggage.

"Alessandro. Back so soon?"

He nodded and handed Nunzia some documents. She handed him a key, and he pivoted toward Patrick. "I love the coast, the sun, and your warm hospitality. I needed a break."

"And Giada?"

From behind Alessandro, Nunzia shook her head and gave Patrick an intense look, trying to discourage him from asking questions.

"She's back in Milan. We're divorcing," Alessandro said matter-of-factly.

"I'm sorry to hear," Patrick said, his eyes widening in surprise.

"It was a long time coming. We are very different."

Patrick agreed, but didn't say anything. "Well, make yourself at home. A bit of relaxation, reading, swimming, and good food is always healing."

"Thank you." Alessandro picked up his bag and walked toward his room. When he was out of sight, Patrick leaned over the counter and whispered to Nunzia, "Poor guy."

"I get the feeling he's relieved."

Patrick chuckled. "True."

"Take good care of him. I like him."

"Me, too," Patrick said. Nunzia raised an eyebrow, and he quickly added, "But not for me."

"I'm watching you," she added.

Nunzia returned to her office, and Patrick walked out onto the deck, surveying the guests to determine who might need attention.

The sun was intense, and people had retreated to the shade of several large umbrellas. The sea was calm. Occasionally, a swell broke against the rocky shoreline, sending a soothing swoosh sound about. People had dozed off, and Patrick picked up empty glasses and plates, walking into the kitchen. He glanced at the stack of wine cases and had an idea. He dialed Pepe on his phone.

"*Pronto*," Pepe answered.

"Pepe, I'm at Nunzia's. Can you make a delivery this morning?"

"You need more wine? I just delivered several cases a week ago."

"It's amazing how quickly it goes," Patrick said, not divulging that they still had plenty in reserve.

"Sure. I can be there in a couple of hours."

"Why don't you plan on having lunch here?"

"I don't want to impose, and I know you all are busy."

"It's a beautiful day. People are off swimming and shopping in Positano."

"Okay."

"And bring your suit, too. You can swim if you like."

Pepe extended the phone away from him and stared at it, wondering what Patrick was up to.

An hour later, Pepe appeared in the lobby with two cases of Benevento wine resting on a dolly. He rang a little bell on the reception counter, and Patrick appeared.

"Pepe, that was quick."

"I didn't have much going on this morning. Where do you want me to put the wine?"

"Follow me."

Patrick led him to a storage area where Pepe unloaded and stacked the cases. They strolled back into the main part of the inn and gazed out at the sparkling water just beyond the lower deck.

"Beautiful day," Pepe remarked.

"Why don't you take a swim? Lunch will be ready at one."

"Where can I change?"

"You can use the staff bathroom. I'll get you a towel."

Pepe changed and came out onto the deck wearing a blue turquoise Speedo, flip-flops, and a towel draped over his shoulder. The sight of him took Patrick's breath away. He was used to seeing Pepe in various stages of dress and undress, but he looked exceptionally delectable as the bright midday sun highlighted the contours of his powerful frame.

"*Bello*," Patrick whispered to him.

Pepe blushed. "See you later for lunch?"

Patrick nodded. Pepe walked to the lower deck, passing Alessandro on the upper deck. Their eyes connected briefly, each realizing they had seen each other before but unable to recall the occasion.

Pepe hung his towel on a hook and dove into the clear blue water. He swam out toward some buoys. With each stroke, he felt tension floating away. The salt water was soothing. He turned on his back and floated in place, gazing up at the clear blue sky.

On the upper deck, Alessandro had lowered the book he was reading and peered toward the water, watching Pepe swim. Patrick approached and asked if there was anything he needed.

"Some mineral water, if you don't mind," Alessandro replied quickly, realizing Patrick may have caught him staring. "By the way, who is that guy swimming? Wasn't he here back in June?"

"He's my cousin. Works on our family vineyard. He just made a delivery."

"Hmm," Alessandro murmured.

"I'll get your water," Patrick said, retreating to the kitchen with a grin on his face.

When he returned, Alessandro was still looking toward the water. Pepe had gotten out, and he was drying himself. Even Patrick had a difficult time keeping focused on his work. The wet fabric of his suit clung to his formidable cock, and his muscular legs and buttocks shimmered in the light. He slipped on his flip-flops and walked to the upper deck.

"Can I change for lunch?" he asked Patrick.

Patrick nodded and followed him into the main part of the inn. He needed to help Franco with lunch.

A short while later, people gathered at umbrella covered tables on the upper deck. Patrick set out carafes of wine, water, and baskets of bread. He had also orchestrated a fake problem – a shortage of tables. Pepe arrived, and Patrick showed him a table. Alessandro arrived shortly thereafter, and Patrick gave the deck a look, as if searching for a suitable place for him to sit.

"Alessandro, I realize there's a problem. I didn't set up the right number of tables. If you will give me a moment, I will go get another table. He then eyed Pepe's table, placed his index finger on his mouth as if in thought, and asked, "Unless you might like to share a table with my cousin."

Alessandro couldn't believe his luck. He tried to conceal his excitement and said, "Sure. I don't mind. It would be nice to have someone to visit with."

Patrick turned to Pepe and said, "Pepe, do you mind if Alessandro shares a table with you. I didn't put out the right number."

"Not at all. *Si accomodi*," Pepe said, gesturing for Alessandro to take a seat.

Patrick pulled up a chair, and Alessandro sat facing Pepe. Patrick circulated amongst the tables, making sure everyone found their place.

"Wine?" Pepe offered as he lifted the carafe over Alessandro's glass.

Alessandro nodded. "I hear this is from your vineyard. It's quite nice."

"Thanks. We are fortunate to have a good piece of land that produces complex wine."

"Who makes the wine?"

"I do."

Alessandro raised a brow in surprise and said, "Congratulations. I'm sure it is an art."

Pepe felt his heart pound in his chest. Most considered him a farmer or a foreman, at best. Alessandro had already recognized his elevated status. Their lunch was off to a good start. "And you? Where are you from?"

"Milan."

"Didn't I see you here a while back?" Pepe inquired.

Alessandro nodded. "I can't get enough of the coast, the sun, the water."

"What do you do?"

"Investment broker."

"Ah," Pepe said. "And for fun?"

"Why don't you think that's fun?" Alessandro pressed, winking at Pepe.

"I don't know. Numbers and charts."

"I like theater, the arts, and literature."

Pepe thought he would pass out on the spot. Fortunately, Patrick arrived with appetizers – grilled vegetables and a small salad. They both took a sip of wine and began to eat.

"What do you like to read?" Pepe inquired.

"A variety of things. Classic works – like the dialogues of Plato. History. I'm reading a biography about Augustus. For fun, I read Paolo Giordano. Curious fellow . . ."

Before Alessandro could finish his sentence, Pepe interjected, "Yes. I know. He's a physicist turned writer."

Alessandro tilted his head in disbelief. He didn't expect the hunky vintner to be up on contemporary Italian literature. "You know him?"

Pepe nodded, taking a bite of his salad.

"I take it you like to read," Alessandro added.

Pepe nodded. "In addition to Paolo Giordano, I like Ella Ferrante, Deborah Harkness, Joël Dicker."

"Do you read Dicker in the original, in French?"

"I try, but I usually revert to the Italian translation."

"Who is Deborah Harkness?"

"She's a historian, a scholar of medicine and magic, but writes fiction."

"I don't know her. I'll have to look her up. I like the esoteric."

Patrick stopped at their table and asked, "Everything good? Do you guys need anything?"

Both smiled. Alessandro said, "All is good. We're discovering that we have a lot of common interests."

"I wondered if that might not be the case. Again, sorry for the inconvenience of having to seat you together."

As Patrick walked to an adjacent table, Pepe followed him with his eyes. Under his breath, he murmured, "Sorry, my ass. You set this up."

"What was that?" Alessandro asked, not making out what Pepe mumbled.

"Oh, nothing. My cousin. He's a nice guy."

"Yes. He's been very understanding and accommodating. He and Nunzia are so warm."

Pepe gave Alessandro a quizzical look, wondering in what sense Patrick had been understanding.

"My wife, or I should say, my former wife, can be a pain."

"Former?"

"I'm in the process of getting a divorce."

"I'm sorry to hear," Pepe said disingenuously, delighted at the news. Now he just needed to confirm Alessandro liked men. It appeared he might, given his earlier wandering eye.

"Thanks. It was a long time coming. We just weren't compatible."

"Kids?"

"No. But I always wanted them. She didn't. And you?"

"Me? Do I have kids?"

Alessandro nodded.

"No, but I would like some. I'm close to my cousin and his husband. They have a son who I adore," Pepe said.

"I might have seen him once before."

"He's five. Cute."

Alessandro nodded. "So, Patrick has a husband?"

"You didn't know?"

"He is warm and friendly, but he and Nunzia are professional and discreet."

"*Scusi*," Pepe said playfully, looking across the terrace at Patrick. "Maybe I said too much."

Alessandro looked off pensively. He was putting pieces of a puzzle together. "So, does Patrick live on the vineyard?"

Pepe nodded.

"And his husband?"

"Zeno. Zeno works in Positano. They live next door to me on the estate."

Alessandro leaned back in his chair and gave Pepe a scrutinizing look. He was dying to ask Pepe if he had a girlfriend or boyfriend, but felt it might be premature and too personal. "But Patrick is American, right?"

"Italian heritage but born in the States."

"How did he end up back here?"

"Long story. His grandparents and parents had all passed. He came to settle their affairs and wanted to identify a man who posed in a picture with his grandfather."

"Did he find him?"

"Yes. It ended up that Zeno's grandfather was Patrick's grandfather's friend. There was a falling out with the patriarch, and Patrick's grandfather emigrated to Boston. When Patrick met Zeno by chance, Patrick recognized the resemblance."

"What was the falling out?"

"Zeno's grandfather wanted to marry Patrick's great aunt. The patriarch wouldn't permit it. He claimed Stefano, Zeno's grandfather, wasn't fit for his daughter since he was an orphan. What no one knew until recent DNA research was that Stefano was the patriarch's illegitimate son."

"Wow! What a story."

"It gets better. I discovered papers in some old books left by Stefano in my house. They were love notes between him and Patrick's grandfather, Roberto."

"So, Zeno's and Patrick's grandfathers were secretly in love. And now Zeno and Patrick are lovers."

"Precisely."

"Amazing. And you? How are you related?"

Pepe froze. Conversation with Alessandro was easy. He was affable, curious, thoughtful, and handsome. He had already tried to conceal his origins with Rocco, to no avail. Perhaps honesty was a better strategy. "I'm adopted. Patrick's cousin, Alberto, is my adopted father and inherited the vineyard. Nunzia is my aunt."

"What a fascinating story."

"A bit crazy, huh?"

"No. It's touching. Love comes full circle."

'A romantic,' Pepe thought to himself. He gave Alessandro another look. In any other context, he would have pegged him as a typical northern Italian businessman. He was tall and lean, with a traditional haircut – although the light breeze coming off the water had tossed a few tufts of dirty blond hair over his forehead. His shoulders were broad and his posture upright, erect, self-composed. He could fully imagine sitting across from him in an office, intimidated by his professional demeanor. But he had seen him earlier in his black Speedo and had been the object of Alessandro's curious eyes. He furtively gazed between the folds of his long-sleeve cotton shirt at the smooth chest that had tanned in the southern Italian sun. Pepe sighed.

Patrick arrived with the main course – a Seabass drizzled with a bright green sauce. "Hmm," Pepe said as he breathed in the pleasant aromas of the dish.

"The food here is amazing," Alessandro noted. "*Grazie*, Patrick."

Patrick smiled, having observed the way Pepe and Alessandro's eyes seemed glued to each other.

"So, where were we?" Alessandro began as he took a bite of his lunch.

"Patrick and Zeno?"

"Yes. And you?" Alessandro went for the jugular. He didn't want to waste time.

Pepe blushed. He wasn't sure why. He still felt some ambiguity about coming out, but he also didn't want anyone to uncover the tangled affections he, Patrick, and Zeno had for one another.

"Me, what?" Pepe replied, not wanting to give up too much too quickly.

"Girlfriend? Boyfriend?"

Pepe looked off evasively and then pivoted back toward Alessandro. "No one at the moment."

Alessandro took a sip of wine to conceal the grin on his face. He was in his own process of coming out, and he detected Pepe might be struggling, too. He'd have to find out more from Patrick and resolved to ask questions later.

"Where does one go here to meet people?"

"Don't ask me," Pepe replied. "I live a quiet life on the farm."

Alessandro looked at Pepe over the top of his glass of wine. While he had the solid body of a farmer, he was too refined to be only that. He had glowing skin, playful dark hair, and alluring eyes. It was clear he was intelligent, thoughtful, and inquisitive. Alessandro felt his cock throb as he imagined undressing Pepe and running his hands down over his muscular torso and into the folds of his shorts.

"And you think I believe that?"

Pepe blushed. "There are some nice music venues in Positano."

"I've heard."

Pepe almost offered to take Alessandro, but decided he needed more information from Patrick first. Both finished their lunches, and Patrick came to pick up their plates. While Patrick stacked them nearby, Pepe stood. "I have to get back to the vineyard," he said.

Patrick glanced at Alessandro and then back at Pepe. "There's no hurry. Relax. Enjoy the sun."

"No. I have to get back. Alberto is waiting for me. Alessandro, it was a pleasure to meet you and share lunch. Maybe I will see you again before you leave." He extended his hand.

"It was nice to meet a fellow bibliophile." Alessandro struggled to come up with a casual but compelling segue, a reason for them to get together. "Maybe you could give me a tour of the vineyard while I'm here."

Pepe nodded. "Sure. Why don't you chat with Patrick and come up with a plan?"

Patrick and Alessandro looked at each other and nodded. Pepe shook Alessandro's hand and retreated to the main building and his car.

Alessandro sat back down and took a long sip of wine. Patrick finished taking care of other tables and returned from the kitchen to find Alessandro reclining on a nearby chaise, taking in the sun.

"Alessandro, anything I can get for you?"

Alessandro opened his eyes. "No. But do you have a moment?"

Patrick nodded and sat on the adjacent chaise.

"I didn't realize you have a partner and a son."

"Pepe must have shared a few things."

"He did. Quite a story."

Suddenly, Patrick began to perspire. He worried Pepe had shared too much. "What did he tell you?"

"About your journey to find your grandfather's friend and your meeting Zeno. I understand you have a son, too. That's impressive, particularly considering southern Italian culture."

"Our family has been very welcoming." Patrick relaxed a bit.

"That's good to hear."

"I have a question."

Patrick rested his chin on the back of his hand, signaling he was ready to listen to Alessandro.

"You know Giada and I are getting a divorce."

"Yes."

"Well, I've been struggling."

"I can imagine it is difficult."

Alessandro paused. He appeared to be deep in thought. "It's not so much a matter of the divorce. It's that I have been trying to make sense of my own life and affections."

"Ah. Yes," Patrick said.

"Do you know what I mean?" Alessandro asked, uncomfortably.

"I think I do. It's never easy, and there are lots of competing practicalities."

"Exactly," Alessandro said excitedly. "For example, I want a family."

"I have one."

"That's why I wanted to talk to you. How does that work?"

"What do you mean?"

"Is it possible to be married to a man and have kids?"

"In Italy, no. In the USA, yes. Zeno and I were fortunate in that a local Italian magistrate officiated at a civil union ceremony, here. In the States, we got married. A local agency worked with us to facilitate Massimo's adoption, but there are all sorts of laws in Italy that make that difficult. We've legalized things regarding Massimo in the States."

Alessandro looked away nervously and wrung his hands. He turned back to Patrick and said, "I think I am gay. I really want to have a family. But it's so hard to be married to a woman and know that I'm not giving her what she needs or deserves."

"And it's not fair to you, either. It's not healthy."

Alessandro furrowed his brow. His indiscretions bothered him. He no longer wanted to live a lie or a double life. "I feel like I'm jumping off a cliff. I don't want to remain married to Giada, but I feel like the gay scene isn't for me."

"As in the straight community, there are all sorts of lifestyles in the gay community. Some prefer being single and hooking up. Others are partnered but open, and others are more traditional and exclusive. There are some who have kids and some who don't. It's all a matter of choice."

"But where do I find someone who shares my values?"

"I think you already did."

"Pepe?"

Patrick smiled. "Yes."

"Do you think he might be interested?"

Patrick glanced across the deck. He didn't want Alessandro to see the grin or excitement on his face. Once composed, he turned to him and said, "I think so. Did you get a good vibe over lunch?"

"Yes. We share a lot of common interests. He mentioned he would like kids. Is he gay?"

"You couldn't tell?"

"I'm not sure I have good gaydar, as I think you call it."

"Pepe is imposing, and it's easy to misread him."

"So, is that a yes?"

"Um-hum."

"So, do you think I could ask him on a date?"

"Why don't you come to Zeno's and my home for dinner? I can show you the vineyard and invite Pepe, too. I think he might respond better to something casual like that. You can see how things unfold."

"I would like that. I'd love to meet your husband and see what your life is like."

"What about the day after tomorrow? Zeno is off."

"Perfect. I'll get directions from you later."

"Well, enjoy the afternoon."

"Thanks for the talk and your understanding."

"My pleasure."

7

Chapter Seven – The Tonic of the Vines

Alessandro paced nervously in front of the mirror in his room, buttoning and unbuttoning the top of his shirt, making sure his hair was just right, spritzing a bit of cologne on his neck, and running his finger along his temples, hoping the creases wouldn't be too obvious.

He slipped his phone into his pocket and headed out the door. Following the instructions Patrick had given him, he took the winding country road up from Praiano through the village of Cava dei Lupi and then onto the gravel road that led to the Benevento estate.

He stopped in front of Patrick's and Zeno's cottage and got out of the car. The sun had set behind the surrounding peaks, and lights inside the house filled the windows with an orange glow. He walked up to the front door, took a deep breath, and knocked.

Zeno came to the door. "You must be Alessandro. Come in. *Benvenuto!*"

"*Piacere,*" Alessandro said, extending his hand.

Massimo ran up behind Zeno and peered up at Alessandro, introducing himself. "*Mi chiamo Massimo.*"

"It's a pleasure to meet you, Massimo." Alessandro extended his hand, and Massimo shook it confidently.

Patrick came up to Zeno's side and leaned forward, giving Alessandro a kiss on his cheek. "Welcome. Come in. You've met Pepe."

Pepe was standing in the middle of the living room. He hadn't decided whether to shake Alessandro's hand or give him a kiss and embrace. He approached Alessandro, who leaned forward and gave Pepe a kiss on his cheek. Pepe said, "Welcome."

"Something to drink?" Zeno offered.

"Some of the excellent Benevento wine, if I may?"

"*Subito,*" Zeno said, retreating to the kitchen to pour everyone a glass.

"Have a seat," Patrick gestured.

Alessandro sat in one of the large easy chairs, Pepe in another, and Massimo and Patrick sat on the sofa. Massimo sipped lemonade, and Pepe nervously reached for some prosciutto on the platter set on the coffee table.

Zeno handed everyone a drink, and Patrick said, "*Salute!* Welcome."

"How's your vacation going?" Pepe jumped in.

"It's been nice. It was the break I needed. Your aunt's inn is so relaxing. She and Patrick take good care of the guests!"

"How much longer will you be there?" Zeno inquired.

"At least another week. I'm in no hurry to go back to Milan."

"Are you able to work remotely?" Patrick asked.

Alessandro nodded. "I manage accounts. I confer with clients over the phone or email. I only have to go into the office occasionally."

"That's convenient," Zeno noted.

"And you, young man," Alessandro said, looking at Massimo. "I understand you are going into first grade this year. And you are Pepe's main helper, right?"

Massimo rocked his legs under him. He nodded, slid off the sofa, and ran into his room. He returned with an instrument. "This is a refractometer. We measure the sugar content of grapes."

"That's why the wine is so delicious!" Alessandro said.

Pepe stared at Alessandro as he interacted with Massimo. He already knew Alessandro wanted kids, and it was apparent he knew how to make them feel important and grown up. He smiled.

Zeno sliced some cheese and took a bite. He scrutinized Alessandro, having heard much about him from Patrick. He made a good first impression. He liked that he paid attention to Massimo - that he was personable and warm. He was also handsome. Patrick had described his stature, complexion, and hair. He had failed to mention his alluring and expressive eyes.

After a short while, Zeno stood and said, "I'll put the final touches on dinner if you guys want to give Alessandro a tour of the vineyard and cellar."

Massimo leaped up and took Alessandro's hand. "Come. I'll show you how we make wine."

Alessandro chuckled, glancing over at Pepe and Patrick.

"Looks like we are taking a tour," Pepe noted.

They walked outside. While the adjacent hills cast the house and vineyard in shade, the sea in the distance shimmered in the late afternoon sunlight. "Breathtaking," Alessandro said as he stared at the horizon.

"We love it," Patrick said as he paused at the edge of the vines stretching off into the distance. "The light changes all the time."

"Let's go this way," Pepe suggested, leading them up the hill to the facility where he and Alberto made wine.

"Who lives there?" Alessandro asked.

"*Zio* Alberto," Massimo chimed in.

"My father, mother, and their kids," Pepe added.

"Beautiful house and setting," Alessandro observed.

"Here's the fermentation equipment," Pepe said as they walked inside the facility. The tall stainless-steel tanks glistened in the overhead lights.

"It's immaculate."

"We set high standards for ourselves," Pepe said.

"What he's not saying is that he is a perfectionist," Patrick commented.

Pepe blushed. He led them deeper inside the structure and downstairs into the lower cellar. "Here are the barrels for aging the wine."

"This seems like a large production."

"It is, although we are more of a boutique estate compared to others. Quality over quantity."

"It's evident," Alessandro noted.

"And here is where we store vintages," Patrick said, pointing to the long room lined with bottles and cases.

"Impressive," Alessandro said. "Until I stayed at the Belvedere, I had never heard of your wine."

"We have more of a local distribution," Pepe observed.

"I'll have to take some home with me."

"That can be arranged," Pepe said with a gleam in his eye.

Alessandro put his hand on Massimo's shoulder and asked, "And young man, what is your role at the vineyard?"

"He's my number one assistant," Pepe interjected quickly.

"Is that right?"

Massimo nodded and said, "You should come to the *vendemmia* and help us. It's a lot of fun, and there's a big luncheon."

"I'm afraid I'm not much of a farmer," Alessandro said.

"Neither is my dad," Massimo noted, glancing up at Patrick. "But he likes the *vendemmia*."

"Sounds like a lot of work," Alessandro suggested.

"It is," Patrick confirmed, laughing.

"It is good for you. It builds character," Pepe noted, pressing Patrick playfully on his arm.

"And sore backs."

Alessandro watched Pepe and Patrick banter back and forth – verbally and physically. He detected an underlying bond and wondered if they had ever been intimate.

Patrick received a text from Zeno. "Dinner is almost ready. Let's head back."

Pepe placed his hand behind Alessandro and led him forward. Alessandro felt goosebumps run up his back as he savored Pepe's solicitous warm touch.

Massimo raced ahead and opened the door for Patrick, Pepe, and Alessandro.

"Wow! It smells incredible in here," Alessandro observed.

"Roast chicken," Zeno announced. "Pepe's recipe."

"You cook?" Alessandro inquired.

"And paints," Patrick added.

Pepe blushed. He helped Massimo get seated and went into the kitchen to bring out platters of vegetables and pasta.

When Pepe was in the kitchen, Alessandro took the opportunity to thank Patrick. "I appreciate the invitation. Pepe seems amazing."

"He is."

"Did you tell him I'm gay?"

"I didn't need to."

"So, is he okay with my being here? It seems contrived – like you're trying to set us up."

"It's a casual dinner on a vineyard. It doesn't have to be anything more."

"Do you invite a lot of hotel guests here?" Alessandro asked, raising his brow.

"Never. You're special," Patrick said, winking at him.

Alessandro began to perspire. Zeno and Pepe came in with food and set platters on the table. Steam rose from the chicken and filled the room with a pleasant aroma. "Everyone have a seat," Patrick commanded. He strolled around the table and filled everyone's glass with wine.

He sat, raised his glass, and said, "*Bevenuto*, Alessandro. We're glad you could join us."

"It's a pleasure to be here. My grandparents had a small family vineyard in the Piemonte region. As a young boy, I remember spending time there, helping with the harvest, and assisting my grandfather."

"Then you should definitely come back for the *vendemmia*," Zeno interjected. "After several of the vineyards complete the harvest, there's a big festival in town."

"Sounds charming. I miss those kinds of events and activities in the countryside."

Patrick nudged Pepe under the table. Pepe glared at him and then turned to Alessandro, saying, "What kind of grapes did your grandparents grow?"

"Nebbiolo."

"And does your family still have the vineyard?" Pepe pressed.

"Unfortunately, no. My father wasn't much into it, and he sold the property. My wife, or I should say my soon to be ex-wife's family, has a vineyard, but she hates it. We never go."

Zeno and Patrick caught each other's attention and nodded imperceptibly. Massimo's head pivoted back and forth as he listened to the adults.

"What brought you to the Belvedere?" Pepe inquired.

"That's an interesting story. I'm not sure if I shared it with Patrick or not. Excuse me if I already told you what happened."

Patrick nodded no. He hadn't heard the story.

"We had booked rooms at the Saraceno in Positano."

"Nice place," Zeno remarked.

"When we arrived, they had overbooked."

"That's unusual," Zeno added.

"They had secured rooms at another place in town, but we weren't impressed with it."

"What did you do?" Pepe inquired.

"Friends of ours had stayed at the Belvedere before. They raved about it. It's not a five-star hotel, as we had imagined for our vacation, but it sounded better than the substitute place. So, we called, and there was a room available."

"Was that when you were here in June?" Patrick asked.

Alessandro nodded.

"Giada didn't seem to like it much," Patrick noted.

"She doesn't like anything. All her friends were in Positano, so she would take the car each day and meet up with them. It made for a very relaxing vacation!" Alessandro said, chuckling.

"And you came back," Patrick noted.

"Things were increasingly uncomfortable back home. The Belvedere is a great place from which to work and soak up some sun. You and Nunzia take good care of guests, and Franco's food is amazing."

"It doesn't hurt that the setting is so spectacular," Patrick added.

"I have to say, it is striking. The coastline views, the crystal-clear water, and the sun-drenched decks are exotic, and the hotel has a classy simplicity to it – white plaster walls, colorful ceramics, and planters filled with herbs."

"We'll have to get you to write our next promotional piece," Patrick said with a large smile.

Zeno nodded as he offered seconds to Alessandro and spooned some vegetables onto Massimo's plate. Pepe remained notably quiet, observing Alessandro and his interaction with the family.

After dinner, dessert, and espresso, Patrick cleared the table. In other circumstances, he would have offered Alessandro a brandy or an amaro, but hoped Pepe might do that.

Visibly nervous, Pepe stood and accompanied Zeno to the kitchen.

"What do you think?" he asked him quietly.

"I like him. What about you?"

"Too good to be true. I don't want to get burned again."

"We know more about him than Giorgio. He seems genuine."

"Should I ask him over for a drink?"

"What do you want to do?" Zeno pressed.

Pepe hesitated and then nodded. He returned to the dining room. Massimo was showing Alessandro his tablet and a book he was reading. Pepe leaned against the wall and smiled at their interaction. Alessandro looked over, and Pepe thought his legs would give way under him. Alessandro's tender eyes conveyed his own excitement at what might be unfolding.

Massimo ran off to his room, and Alessandro said to Patrick, "Thanks for dinner and the invitation. I'll see you back at the inn tomorrow?"

Zeno stepped out of the kitchen and said, "Alessandro, it was a delight to meet you. Ordinarily, we'd offer you an after-dinner drink, but it's Massimo's bedtime, and I have an early shift tomorrow. I hope we will see you again."

Alessandro was about to speak when Pepe cleared his throat and interjected, "Alessandro, if you aren't too tired, I could offer you a drink at my place and show you some of my art."

"That would be nice."

Patrick gave Alessandro an embrace and kiss on the cheek, as did Zeno. Pepe and he walked outside and down the road to Pepe's place.

8

Chapter Eight – Magic

"Come in," Pepe said as he opened the door for Alessandro. Alessandro paused just inside the door. He pivoted in place with his mouth agape. "My God. It's stunning."

Pepe led him farther into the space and said, "Zeno's grandfather lived here a long time ago. He had a lot to do with the bones of the place. I just gave it some cosmetic touches."

"I like the historic wood beamed structure, stucco walls, dark tile floors, and the contemporary but comfortable furniture, rugs, and lamps. And the art!"

Pepe blushed. He followed Alessandro, who approached a seascape on one of the walls.

"You did this?" Alessandro asked.

Pepe nodded. "My father paints, and I learned a lot from him."

"Do you have a studio?"

"Yes. This way," Pepe said as he turned on more lights and led him to the back of the house.

"Wow! What a nice space — the bookcases and easels and sitting area."

"This is where I read, think, and create."

"Is this one you're working on?" Alessandro asked as he approached a large canvas set on a wooden easel.

Pepe walked up behind him and breathed in Alessandro's intoxicating cologne. He gazed at the nape of his neck and followed the contours of his shoulders under the crinkly linen fabric of his shirt. Alessandro turned toward Pepe, and their eyes connected. For a protracted moment, neither said a word. Both knew they were falling under each other's spell.

Pepe pierced the silence. "Yes. It's a group of fishing boats moored by Nunzia's inn. Maybe you've seen them. I wanted to capture the moment when the light is more angular and magical."

"Hmm. Amazing."

"That drink I offered? A brandy or an amaro?"

"Brandy would be nice."

Pepe retreated to the kitchen, poured them both a glass and returned to the living room, inviting Alessandro to take a seat.

"Cheers!" Pepe offered.

"*Salute!*" Alessandro said in return.

"It was nice to spend time at Zeno's and Patrick's. I have to say, they are very inspiring."

"They are special!"

Both wanted to say that they wanted what Patrick and Zeno had. But both realized they needed to work up to that. It was premature to declare their interests so soon.

"How long have they lived here?"

"I think it's been five or six years. They met when Patrick first came. They adopted Massimo a year later."

"You all seem very close."

Pepe took a drink of the brandy to conceal his apprehension that Alessandro might have detected underlying affections. He then said, "We are all family, and we get along nicely."

"Massimo is quite the character!"

"He has picked up all the best traits of Zeno, Patrick, and Alberto."

"And you," Alessandro said, pointedly.

"I don't know about that."

"He looks up to you."

"I'm *Zio* Pepe to him."

"You mentioned yesterday that you wanted kids," Alessandro observed.

"Yes."

"But?"

Pepe looked off across the room. He pivoted back to Alessandro and took a long sip of the brandy. "It doesn't seem to be in the cards."

"Why not?"

"It's complicated." Pepe realized they were speeding quickly to very personal matters. He felt relaxed and comfortable with Alessandro, but wasn't sure how much to share.

There was a long pause. Alessandro said, "Can I use the restroom?"

Pepe nodded.

Alessandro retreated to the bathroom and returned. He took a seat next to Pepe on the sofa. It had been a strategic move. He gazed into Pepe's eyes.

Pepe didn't overlook the gesture. He smiled warmly.

"Complicated. How?"

"Oh. The matter of children?"

"Yes."

"Well, this isn't exactly where people want to settle and start a family."

Pepe's gender neutrality threw Alessandro off. Maybe he would have to be more direct. "It seems ideal to me."

Pepe's heart began to pound. Alessandro wasn't exactly his type, but he was handsome, and the image of him sitting on the chaise at Nunzia's inn was memorable and alluring. He recalled Alessandro's smooth chest and firm pecs. He had muscular legs and full, round buttocks. Most importantly, he had a killer smile and dreamy eyes. Could he fall in love with him?

Pepe reached his hand over and placed it playfully on Alessandro's thigh. "You're too kind," Pepe said. "It's rather boring."

"Urban life is overrated. As I said over dinner, I miss going to my grandparents' vineyard. When I was a boy, I couldn't wait to leave the city, work the field, enjoy hearty meals, and listen to the adults."

Pepe tilted his head, incredulous as to what Alessandro was saying.

Alessandro continued, "You have your art and books. You are minutes to the coast and to Naples, with all it offers. And you have a nice close-knit family that adores you."

Pepe blushed.

"And I can see why," Alessandro added, running his hand over Pepe's shoulder.

Pepe froze.

Alessandro set his glass on the table and leaned toward Pepe. He traced his finger over Pepe's brow. "*Quanto sei bello!*" he said, letting his hand rest on Pepe's chest.

"You're handsome, too," Pepe said tenderly, pressing his hand between Alessandro's legs.

Alessandro gave Pepe a warm kiss.

Pepe savored the sweetness of Alessandro's lips and kissed him back.

"Is this okay? Are you okay?" Alessandro asked.

Pepe's heart skipped a beat. No one had ever asked him that. It was one of the sexiest things a man had ever said to him.

Pepe nodded. He felt his cock stiffen. He reached over and unbuttoned Alessandro's shirt, sliding his hand over the warm smooth skin underneath. Alessandro shook nervously. Pepe noticed.

"Are you okay?" Pepe asked.

"It's all kind of new to me," Alessandro replied. There had been quick hook ups over the years – fast, rough, and thoughtless. The idea that someone wanted to make love to him sent adrenaline coursing through his body.

Intuitively, Pepe pulled back and held Alessandro's hand. "We all carry scars."

Alessandro nodded pensively. Then he said, "Your hands are so warm."

Pepe reached over and slid Alessandro's shirt off, running his hands over his lean, round shoulders. He took hold of his upper arm and squeezed it affectionately. He glanced down and noticed Alessandro was aroused.

Alessandro took hold of the bottom of Pepe's pullover and lifted it. Pepe slipped out of the shirt and reclined on the back of the sofa as Alessandro traced his hand over Pepe's hardening pecs. "So delicious," Alessandro murmured as he leaned forward and ran his hot, wet tongue around the contours of Pepe's chest.

Alessandro pressed himself against Pepe's chest and could hear his heartbeat underneath. Pepe reached around him and gave him an affectionate embrace, running his hand down his back and into the loose waist of his jeans. He could feel the hardness of Alessandro's sex pressing against his pelvis.

Alessandro gave Pepe a deep, ardent kiss. Pepe savored the feel of Alessandro's tongue and the intimacy it promised. For the first time in his life, even though Alessandro was on top of him, he didn't feel cornered or alarmed. Alessandro extended his arms and ran his hand through Pepe's thick, dark hair. Pepe moaned as he felt the solidity of Alessandro's body extended over him and his legs wrapped around his waist.

Pepe pressed Alessandro to the side and unzipped his jeans. He reached his hand inside and took hold of Alessandro's long, engorged cock. He stroked it, and Alessandro let out a cry of delight.

With his other hand, Pepe unzipped his own jeans. His erection sprung free of his undershorts. Pepe took both of their moist cocks in his hand and massaged them, giving Alessandro a protracted kiss at the same time.

Pepe lifted a knee over Alessandro and straddled him, continuing to stroke them feverishly. Their skin became hot, and Pepe felt himself grow increasingly aroused. He could hardly contain himself and let go of their cocks, pressing his rock-hard sex between Alessandro's legs.

Alessandro gazed up at the handsome man towering over him – at Pepe's tightening pecs, at his gleaming abdomen, and at the muscular thighs clutching him. He took hold of his own moist sex and stroked it. But he started to tremble. He took a deep breath and closed his eyes. He felt Pepe's thick, engorged cock press against him. He wanted to enjoy it, to relish the hunger of Pepe's body consuming him, but he couldn't. In a desperate fit, he twisted his body and threw Pepe onto his side.

Pepe clung to Alessandro's torso, pressing and massaging his wet chest. He felt Alessandro's sex against his own and almost came. He reached down and took hold of them both. He felt the sensitive end of his penis vibrate and tingle as it slid against

Alessandro's. He felt a warm wave rise from his legs and explode in his hand and onto Alessandro. As Pepe gave one final squeeze, Alessandro let go and came in a dramatic climax, too, his body writing with pleasure.

They both collapsed on the sofa and struggled to catch their breaths. When both were calm, Pepe said, "Wow!"

"Hmm," Alessandro murmured, fearful that perhaps Pepe had been disappointed. Pepe clearly wanted to fuck him, but it was too traumatic. He had hoped coming out and embracing his sexual desires would have healed troubling thoughts, but his body carried those memories, and he shook uncontrollably. Relieved that at least they had both come, Alessandro reached for his jeans and slipped them on. Pepe slipped on his undershorts and reached to the side table for his brandy. He took a long sip, staring at Alessandro.

Alessandro reached for his glass and finished it in one final gulp. "I should probably get back to the inn."

"Stay."

Alessandro didn't respond. Pepe wasn't sure if he was pondering the invitation or thinking of an excuse. Finally, he said, "It's premature."

"Not if you know what you want," Pepe said in retort.

Alessandro's eyes watered. Since marrying Giada, he had been fighting an internal battle, one he wasn't sure he was winning. For the first time in his life, he was optimistic that he might find a compatible male partner and be able to start a family. He couldn't believe his luck.

Pepe inched up to him and ran his finger over Alessandro's brow. "It's funny. I didn't see this coming."

Alessandro shook his head no. He hadn't either.

Pepe stood. He took Alessandro's hand and helped him up. He led him back to the bedroom, where he removed his jeans. He pulled back the covers of the bed and helped Alessandro in. Pepe walked around the other side of the bed, slid off his shorts, and climbed in. He reached his arms around Alesandro and pulled him close. They both fell into a peaceful sleep.

9

Chapter Nine – All On The Table

Zeno strolled into the kitchen and turned on the espresso machine. He glanced out of the window and noticed Alessandro's car was still parked in front of their house. He ran back to the bedroom and nudged Patrick. "Alessandro spent the night with Pepe."

"What?" Patrick asked groggily.

"Get up. Alessandro is still at Pepe's."

"Leave them be."

"Should we invite them for breakfast?"

"Would you want to do the walk of shame to your neighbor's house?"

Zeno gave Patrick a quizzical look. "Walk of shame?"

"It's an American expression. They will be embarrassed. They don't need or want to come here."

"But I'm curious."

"We can get details later."

"Get up!"

Patrick slid out of bed, put on some shorts and sandals, and walked to the kitchen. Zeno followed him. Massimo had risen and was spreading Nutella on a croissant.

"*Buongiorno, Massimo!*" Patrick said.

"Alessandro had a sleepover with *Zio* Pepe," Massimo remarked.

"Yes. They are good friends," Zeno noted, pushing buttons on the machine to make Patrick an espresso. While doing so, he continued to peer out of the window.

Soon, Alessandro exited Pepe's house and walked to his car. Zeno retreated from the edge of their kitchen but watched from inside. Alessandro got into the car and sped off.

Soon, Pepe walked out of his house and strolled up the hill. He knocked on the door and let himself in. Everyone stared at him.

"What?" he began.

"Spill."

"I don't know what you mean?"

"We want details. How did it go?"

"I'm going to need some coffee," Pepe said to Zeno.

Zeno made him a double espresso and set it in front of him. Zeno said, "Well?"

"It was nice. He is nice."

"Is that it?"

Pepe nodded toward Massimo, not sure how much he should share in his presence. "Later," he said.

"Preview?" Patrick interjected.

"It felt very comfortable, as if we already knew each other. It was very odd. He's not my type. At least I didn't think so."

"Hmm," Patrick murmured as he sipped his coffee and pulled off a piece of croissant.

"How did you leave off?" Zeno inquired.

"We're having lunch together in Amalfi."

"Already?" Patrick asked with a raised brow.

"It's not like we have a lot of time. He will have to go back to Milan soon."

"Okay," Patrick said. He looked at his watch and realized he had a late morning shift at the inn. He would get a chance to question Alessandro, too.

"What did you all think?" Pepe asked.

"We liked him," Massimo expressed before the adults had a chance to chime in.

Everyone laughed.

"Why?" Pepe asked Massimo.

"He likes vineyards," Massimo replied.

"You remember that?" Zeno asked him.

Massimo nodded. "And he likes you."

"How do you know?"

"You had a sleepover."

Pepe turned red. He realized kids didn't sexualize things, but the fact that Massimo knew he spent the night with Alessandro embarrassed him.

"And you guys?" Pepe asked, looking at Zeno and Patrick.

They looked at each other. Patrick began, "He seems nice, in an unassuming way. He's thoughtful and asks questions and seems to share a lot of your interests. But it's all about chemistry."

Pepe looked off as if in thought. He quickly stood and said, "I have to go. I have some chores to do before lunch. See you later!"

Zeno reached over and gave Pepe a hug. "*Buona fortuna!*"

"*Grazie*," he replied and left.

Several hours later, Pepe pulled up to Nunzia's inn. Alessandro was waiting in the front and waved to him. He stood and got into the passenger seat of the car, and Pepe sped off.

"*Ciao*," Pepe said in a warm, solicitous voice.

Alessandro ran his hand along Pepe's thigh and said, "It's nice to see you again so soon!"

Pepe breathed in the familiar cologne Alessandro wore, one he had resisted washing off earlier in the morning. It had already become familiar and charged with memories.

Alessandro gave a protracted look at Pepe as he drove - at the contours of his chest so pronounced under the soft fabric of his pullover, at the shadow of a beard lining his angular jaw and circling his delicious lips, at the playfulness of his dark hair, and at the deep-set adorable eyes glancing over at him from time to time. Pepe grinned like a boy going off to play with his best friend.

Alessandro leaned back in the seat and took a deep breath. In his wildest imagination, he would not have visualized sitting so close to one of the sexiest men he had ever met, holding his hand, and driving down the romantic Amalfi Coast.

"Do you have a favorite place in Amalfi?"

"Not really. There's a café there called Zeno's. We can have a drink and then stroll through the center of the city. There are a lot of restaurants. Why do you like the Amalfi Coast so much?" Pepe asked.

"It's often cold and gray in Milan. It's a wonderful place to take in the sun. I like the dramatic coastline, the beautiful water, and the handsome men!"

"I thought this was all new to you."

"I have eyes."

Pepe pointed two fingers at his eyes and then pointed them back at Alessandro. "I'm watching you!"

"No need to worry. There's nothing better to look at!"

Pepe blushed. He realized he was Alessandro's type. He wished Alessandro was more his type, but he was growing on him. He visualized them in bed together - Alessandro's formidable cock resting against his side, the curve of Alessandro's back giving way to firm, round buttocks, and his long, powerful legs that found their way between and over his own.

Soon, they pulled into Amalfi. Pepe found a parking space, and they walked to Café Zeno.

"This is not a common name. Any connection with your Zeno?"

"Years ago, Patrick thought there was a psychic one, destiny he calls it."

"How so?"

"I think he was having doubts about Zeno and came to Amalfi to think. The name of the bar hit him over the head."

"The universe has a way of doing that," Alessandro said.

"Not you, too."

"What do you mean?"

"Are you into the esoteric?"

"Aren't we all? You know, us Italians?"

"Yes. But I haven't met many guys who admit it."

They approached the bar and ordered drinks. They sat at a small table overlooking the busy pedestrian area of the city. "*Salute!*" they said to each other as they raised their glasses.

"To destiny," Alessandro added.

Pepe nodded and smiled.

"So, why didn't we go to the restaurant where Zeno works in Positano?"

"Are you kidding? Zeno would be hovering over us like a mother hen."

"It's cute, the two of them."

"Yeah, they're cute alright."

"I have to say, it's rather unique. Their relationship, Massimo, you."

Pepe froze. He took a long sip of his drink.

"What's wrong?"

"Nothing," Pepe said, saving information about their past for a later conversation.

Alessandro finished his drink. "Shall we?"

Pepe nodded. They paid their bill and strolled through the busy center of town. The massive steps leading up to the cathedral loomed before them. "It's such a historic town," Alessandro remarked.

"Many tourists overlook it. They gravitate to Positano or Ravello, but Amalfi is where the power and money were hundreds of years ago."

"Are you from here?"

"I'm not sure. I was in the orphanage in Salerno."

"Have you ever tried to look up your biological parents?"

"No. I'm not interested. Alberto and Maria are my parents. *Basta così.*"

"What about this place?" Alessandro said as they paused in front of a trattoria.

Pepe studied the menu and looked at the terrace full of tables. The food looked good. "Yeah. Let's try it."

They walked to the maître d' and asked for a table. He gave them one off to the side, and they took seats, ordering a carafe of local wine.

"So," Alessandro opened.

Pepe wrung his hands nervously and looked away evasively. He knew what was on the table.

"*Senti*, listen," Alessandro continued. "I know this may be rash, but I've never met anyone like you before."

The waiter appeared at the table, asking if they wanted to order. Without giving it much thought, Alessandro chose *scallopine al limone*.

Pepe looked at him and said, "That's one of my favorites!" He looked up and nodded to the waiter. "Me, too."

The waiter asked, "Side dish – perhaps *risotto*? *Risotto ai funghi porcini?*"

Both nodded.

The waiter left the table. Pepe remained unsettled. He cleared his throat and said, "Alessandro. I have to be honest. I had a bad experience with someone recently, and I'm on guard."

"I get that. Guys can be pigs!"

Pepe sighed. "You're married."

"Getting a divorce."

"But you're still married. This is all new to you."

"I realize that. This may sound overly sentimental, but I have been waiting for you my whole life."

Pepe's eyes widened. Alessandro was moving quickly.

"Sorry," Alessandro added, noticing Pepe's alarm. "I'm not young anymore."

"How old are you?"

Alessandro fidgeted with his napkin and said, "Forty-two."

"I'm forty. We're still young."

"At any rate, I have been thinking about this moment my whole life."

"*Spiegami* – explain."

"I married, thinking Giada – who is beautiful – would inspire me to overcome my tendencies."

"Did it work?"

"What do you think?"

Pepe gave a slight nod no.

"Her family was powerful and influential, and I got sucked into the thrill of it all. But I always wanted a family, and a home, and something less flashy and more down-to-earth. I also knew I was attracted to men."

"That must have been difficult."

"It was. I tried to make it work, but we were unhappy. At least I know I was, and I think Giada was, too."

"So, what happened next?"

"We fought more and grew distant. She caught me once with a guy and grew irate. We went to a counselor. The counselor helped me embrace my orientation."

"Giada must have been furious."

"She was, although it gave her permission to have her own affairs."

"And now?"

"We've decided we each need to go our separate ways."

"That's good."

"So that's what brings me to you. I have always wanted someone who valued family, wanted kids, was handsome, unassuming, and yet educated and artistic. You were in all of my dreams. Sorry. I know that may be too sentimental!"

"No. I'm stunned and flattered. I never imagined meeting someone like you, either."

"Where do we go with this?"

The waiter returned with their meals. "*Buon appetito*," both said to each other as they began to eat.

Pepe took a bite of the scallopine and moaned, "This is delicious!"

"*Si, veramente!*"

Pepe finished a bite, took a sip of wine, and then cleared his throat. "Alessandro. I have to share something with you. I want everything to be on the table. No surprises."

Alessandro put his fork down and looked up at Pepe with alarm.

"I just came out last year. I guess I've known for a while, and had a few experiences, but I kept hoping I might find the right woman. No one wanted to settle down with me on the farm. In retrospect, I realize they probably sniffed out my conflicted feelings."

Alessandro smiled.

"I went with Zeno, Patrick, and Massimo to Disney World in Florida last winter."

"Wow! I've always wanted to go."

Pepe smiled, but then turned serious and continued his story. "While we were there, we kind of got involved."

Alessandro tilted his head quizzically.

Pepe hesitated. Then he said, "We are all close. We had to share a bed and, well, things happened."

Alessandro's eyes widened.

"We experimented with the idea of becoming a throuple."

"A throuple?"

"A couple, but with three people."

"Ah."

"It didn't work."

"Why not?"

"We all love each other. But I felt like I wasn't an equal partner. As an orphan, that bothered me."

"So, you aren't involved now?"

"No."

Alessandro sighed. "I'm glad to hear that."

"But."

Alessandro grew concerned.

"We love each other. There's a lot of sexual tension, but I am committed to finding my own relationship. I have to say, until now, I had been discouraged."

Alessandro smiled, realizing he checked all the boxes. But his smile turned to a look of concern as Pepe paused. "But?" Alessandro interjected.

"There are no buts. Despite setbacks, I decided to remain true to my dream. Suddenly, you showed up."

"It is kind of amazing."

"Yes. But you live in Milan."

"Minor detail."

"Not really."

"It is. I can work from anywhere."

"But your home is in the north."

"I don't have anything holding me there."

"But your work."

"Again, I can work remotely."

"It is quiet here. It's not that interesting," Pepe noted.

"You seem busy, and you have a rich life."

"You're persistent."

"Wouldn't you be if you were in my shoes?" Alessandro said, smiling hungrily at Pepe.

Pepe turned red and sliced the veal on his plate. Alessandro did the same, placing a morsel in his mouth — all the while staring at Pepe.

"When do you have to go back?"

"I have some meetings in two weeks. But I can come back after that. Or you can visit Milan."

"Things are busy here. I have a lot of work."

Silently, they finished their meals. Pepe's head was turning with ideas, and he was fighting the urge to convey them. They ordered espressos and strolled through town. Neither said much. Finally, Pepe said, "Are you ready to go back?"

Alessandro said, "Sure."

They found Pepe's car and drove along the coastal road. As they neared Praiano, Alessandro said, "Do you want to hang out on the deck or go for a swim?"

"I have some chores on the estate."

Alessandro turned sullen. Pepe pulled up in front of Nunzia's inn. There was an awkward silence between them. Pepe placed his hand on Alessandro's knee and looked into his eyes.

"Come on. Stay. Let's have a drink on the terrace."

Pepe knew a drink on the terrace was not what Alessandro had on his mind. Pepe shook his head no. "Sorry, I have to get back to the vineyard."

"When can I see you again?" Alessandro pressed.

"I'll call you later, and we can make plans."

Alessandro feared Pepe was having second thoughts. Nevertheless, he leaned forward and gave him a kiss.

Pepe kissed him back forcefully, ardently. He ran his hand through Alessandro's hair and down his back. He savored the firmness of Alessandro's chest against his own and felt his body become warm and aroused. He then extracted himself from their embrace. The wetness of their kiss lingered on his lips, and as he stared into Alessandro's eyes, he felt his skin tingle and his cock stiffen.

"Sorry. I will call you later."

Encouraged by their farewell embrace, Alessandro got out of the car, holding Pepe's hand as long as he could. He waved to him, and Pepe sped off.

Instead of going to the vineyard, Pepe drove to Positano. It was four in the afternoon, and he knew Zeno would be taking it easy, serving drinks to the beach crowd. He parked his car and walked down the hill to the restaurant bar.

The smell of the salt air and the sound of swells crashing on the shore were soothing. Scantily clad tourists reclined in the sun with a few gathered at the bar, sipping drinks. Zeno noticed Pepe walk up and gave him a worried look.

"What's wrong?" Zeno asked as Pepe took a seat.

"I need to talk."

"Problems with Alessandro?"

Pepe didn't answer at first. Then he hesitatingly said, "No. And that's the problem."

"I don't get it."

"It's all perfect."

"That's great," Zeno said excitedly.

"I don't want to be surprised again."

"Take your time. Get to know him."

"It's moving too quickly."

"You've had one date, dinner with us, and a sleepover. He's got to go back to Milan soon. Take your time."

Pepe started to shake. Zeno poured him a glass of wine and slid it toward him. Pepe took hold of the glass and took a long sip.

"What do you think of him?" Pepe inquired.

"He seems nice."

"Is that all?"

"I don't know him."

"But you have good intuition. What do you think?"

"He's down to earth and not pretentious. He likes kids and interacted well with Massimo. He seems to appreciate the countryside and the vineyard. Those are all good things, right?"

Pepe nodded, but it was clear he still wanted Zeno to continue.

"What about the physical part?" Zeno asked.

"That's what's got me worried."

"Why?"

"He's handsome."

"Yes. But?"

"I always visualized someone different - southern, darker, more muscular."

"Pay attention to that. Maybe he's compatible personally, but not physically. That could be a problem later."

"But he's growing on me."

"Maybe that's good. Infatuation doesn't lead to the best decisions."

"What if we see more of each other and it doesn't click?"

"Then you deal with it."

Pepe looked off pensively across the beach. He realized he had never been in a similar situation. His past relationships had always ended when someone else told him it wasn't working. He worried he might be the one to bolt.

"I've been thinking. What if I asked him to spend time with me?"

"You mean at your place?"

Pepe nodded.

"How much time?" Zeno asked with some alarm.

"I don't know. Enough to figure out if there's enough chemistry. He's got to go back to Milan soon. Maybe he could hang out at my place until then."

"Are you sure about that? That's a lot of time together quickly."

"I know. Bad idea."

"No. It might not be a bad idea, but it is rather hasty."

"I've had enough life experiences to know what I want."

"An early move-in can make people panic," Zeno advised.

"But this has an exit strategy. Alessandro can always head back to the north."

"Are you sure about this?"

Pepe shook his head no. "But what do I have to lose?"

"Nothing, my dear!" Zeno gave Pepe a warm smile.

Out of the blue, Pepe said, "I've got to go."

Pepe walked away from the bar, and Zeno yelled, "Hey! You forgot something!" Zeno puckered his lips. "You and Alessandro may become lovers, but I'm still your sexy in-law, and I get a kiss!"

Pepe kissed Zeno quickly and walked briskly up the walkway toward his car. He drove back to the vineyard and took care of chores.

Later that evening, he fretted over how to broach things with Alessandro. Nervously, he dialed his number.

"*Pronto*," Alessandro responded.

"Alessandro. Sorry about this afternoon. I had a lot of work lined up. I would have loved to have stayed."

"No problem. I enjoyed lunch together."

"I'm calling to see if I might join you for lunch at the inn tomorrow?"

"That would be wonderful. We can hang out on the terrace, swim, visit."

"I'll come just before lunchtime. *Ciao*."

"*À presto*."

10

Chapter Ten – Invitation

Pepe pulled up to Nunzia's inn and walked through the lobby. He wore shorts, a tee shirt, and flip-flops. He noticed Alessandro reclining on a chaise at the edge of the terrace. There was an empty lounge next to him. He walked over.

"*Ciao*," Alessandro said with a big smile as he noticed Pepe standing over him. "Take a seat. I saved it for you."

Pepe adjusted the back and sat down. He reached over and furtively grazed Alessandro's hand. Although other guests were dozing, he wanted to be discreet. "How are you doing?"

"Better, now that you are here."

"What are you reading?" Pepe inquired, glancing at the book resting provocatively on Alessandro's crotch.

"I'm embarrassed to say. Plato's *Symposium*."

"Why embarrassed?"

"I don't know. Who goes on vacation to the coast and reads ancient philosophy?"

"I think it's cute."

Alessandro blushed.

"Why the *Symposium?*" Pepe pressed him.

"Different theories on the nature of love."

"And what have you concluded?"

"It's complicated."

"How so?"

Suddenly, Patrick approached. "Pepe. I didn't see you come in." Patrick leaned down and gave Pepe a kiss on his cheek. "Can I get you guys something to drink?"

Alessandro and Pepe glanced at each other. Simultaneously, they both said, "A double espresso."

Everyone chuckled. Patrick said, "Right away." He retreated to the kitchen.

"Where were we?" Pepe interjected.

"Boring philosophy."

"It's not boring. So, what have you extracted from Plato?"

"Love is complicated. We often consider sexual desire to be base, carnal, lacking any noble qualities," Alessandro began.

"But?"

"Well, sometimes it is."

"Granted."

"But often it leads us to things that are important for our development, for authenticity."

"An example?"

"I used to think my attraction to men was dirty, something to fight, something that led me astray. But I grew to realize it was my body's way of guiding me to my authentic self."

"I can relate."

Alessandro chuckled. "But sometimes those desires feel more lustful and end up being little more than a form of self-gratification."

Pepe blushed. "How do we know the difference?"

"That's a good question, and one that Plato explores. In some sense, eros leads us to people who represent the beautiful, the noble, the excellent. People challenge us to grow. Maybe eros has its own mind – a kind of attraction that brings us to people who are good for us."

Pepe pondered his attraction to Giorgio, and then to Alessandro. Was it all just random? He was attracted to Giorgio only to discover his duplicity. Could Alessandro be equally disappointing or, if not, simply an accidentally fortuitous outcome? Or – were the fates involved, as Plato and Socrates might have considered?

"But what happens when things don't work out?"

"Maybe eros teaches us something in the process," Alessandro suggested.

Patrick arrived with their espressos. "Enjoy," he said as he set the cups down on the small table between them.

"Thanks, Patrick," Alessandro said. Pepe nodded.

Both sipped their coffee. Pepe gazed out at the still blue sea. There was little wind and a bit of haze. It would be a warm day. He turned toward Alessandro and observed his smooth chest growing moist in the sun. He recalled their bodies gliding over each other and grew aroused. He realized he had desires for Alessandro. They weren't of the same intensity as those he felt for Giorgio or Patrick or Zeno. He wondered what that meant.

"Are you reading anything these days?" Alessandro asked Pepe.

"Paolo Giordano. *The Solitude of Prime Numbers*."

"I love that book."

"I've read it before, too. I felt like it was worth reading again."

Alessandro recalled the premise of the book – two misfits that destiny brings together later in life and where hidden emotions come to the surface. He wondered if he and Pepe were like prime numbers, and if so, could they ever couple? He liked his solitude, and he imagined Pepe did, too.

"What do you think of it?" Alessandro asked.

"It's a haunting story – as if a force greater than the two characters is at work."

Alessandro was dying to say, 'you mean, like us?' but he refrained. It was clear that the same dynamic was at work, and it floated unspoken in the salty air of the Italian coast. Alessandro finished his espresso and reclined his head on the back of the chaise, closing his eyes. "I love it here," he murmured.

It was rare that Pepe took the time to relax in the sun or take a swim. He stood and peered toward the water. "I'm going to jump in," he declared.

"I'll hang here."

Pepe walked to the lower terrace and then leaped into the water. There were no waves, and the water was crystal clear. He dove and skimmed the rocky bottom, spotting a seahorse feeding on some algae. He surfaced and then floated on his back, taking in the blue sky, the irregular coastline, and the verdant hillsides hovering above Praiano.

He felt a flutter in his stomach contemplating the overtures he kept rehearsing in his mind – an invitation for dinner, an overnight, or something more protracted.

He swam to the edge of the deck and climbed out of the water, making his way back to Alessandro. He reached for a towel and draped it on the chaise. Pepe sat down and reclined. Alessandro could hardly contain himself – Pepe's muscular wet chest gleamed in the sun, and his Speedo left little for the imagination as his large, thick cock pressed against the wet fabric.

"How's the water?"

"Heavenly. Why don't you go in?"

"I will later."

"Have you been working while you are here?"

"A little," Alessandro replied. "I took some time off."

"And Giada? Does she work?"

"No. She comes from money. She's meeting with designers to go over plans to renovate the apartment."

"Your apartment?"

"It will be hers after the divorce. It was part of the settlement."

"And you?" Pepe asked.

"I found another place. It's nice. It's in the center of town, near my office, with lots of conveniences nearby."

"I've never been to Milan."

"You'll have to come."

Pepe realized lots of assumptions were being made.

"This guy she caught you with. Was he someone you knew?" Pepe wanted to do his homework and figured now was as good a time as ever.

"Someone I hooked up with on an app."

"Oh," Pepe said, relieved that at least he wasn't a boyfriend. "Was he cute?"

"Not really. His profile picture had been doctored."

Pepe chuckled. "I am not very experienced in that arena. I hear all sorts of stories."

Alessandro was reassured by Pepe's remark. He hoped Pepe wasn't linking up with a lot of guys. He said, "It's hard to meet people the old fashion way."

"You mean at bars?"

Alessandro nodded.

"I imagine it is a bit easier in Milan than it is here."

"What about Naples?" Alessandro inquired.

"It's very provincial. You have to know somebody or be from there, otherwise it is easy to get into trouble."

"I've always wanted to visit the museums there."

Pepe swallowed hard. Memories of the trip with Giorgio were bittersweet. "Maybe we can go while you are here."

"That would be nice."

They continued to chat until Patrick rang a bell, signaling time for lunch. People stirred from their naps, books, or phones. Pepe and Alessandro slipped on shorts and tee shirts and took seats at a small table. Patrick placed a carafe of wine in front of them and winked at them both. Dario showed up with a mixed salad.

"*Posso?*" Alessandro asked if he could dress the salad, pointing at the oil and vinegar cruets.

Pepe nodded.

Alessandro served them each, and they began to eat. "Hmm," Pepe noted. "So, you're a cook, too?"

"Dressing salad hardly constitutes a skill. But I do cook. *Osso buco* is my speciality."

"Do you make it with white wine and chicken stock or red wine and beef stock?"

"White wine and chicken. I'm from the north. We prefer light sauces."

"Well, that's a deal breaker," Pepe said, trying to add levity to what he knew would be a momentous discussion soon.

"And you? Zeno mentioned your chicken recipe. You must cook."

"I try," Pepe said, realizing as he spoke that Patrick had come up behind them.

"Don't be fooled, Alessandro. Pepe's one of the best cooks in the region."

"Well, well, well. Another hidden talent."

Pepe glared at Patrick. "Don't you have other tables to serve?"

Patrick set the platter of grilled pork chops and roast potatoes on the table. "*Buon appetito*," he said to them.

"*Grazie*," they both said in unison.

"I love how they season things here. Look at how perfectly this is grilled. Franco creates a nice caramelized glaze on the outside, but the meat is moist."

"And the potatoes are Patrick's recipe. Nice and crispy," Pepe added.

"I didn't realize."

Pepe observed Alessandro slice into the chop. He cleared his throat.

"So, how is Giada with the divorce and your coming out?"

Alessandro shifted nervously in his chair. "On the surface, she's been cooperative. She always has a smile, but it often conceals underlying hostility."

Pepe grew alarmed.

"Have you signed papers?"

"We have a meeting with lawyers just before *Ferragosto*."

"A holiday event, then!"

Alessandro didn't smile. He looked troubled. "I feel so bad."

"You said she was having her own affairs."

Alessandro nodded. "Everything is about appearances. Her parents aren't happy with our splitting up."

"If so, they're probably not happy with a gay son-in-law."

"True." Alessandro sliced his pork chop and took a bite pensively.

"She didn't want to have children?"

Alessandro shook his head.

"How did that sit with her parents?"

"Not well."

"Why didn't she want them?"

"I think she feared it would interfere with her lifestyle."

"How did you meet?"

"At a party thrown by my boss."

"Who approached whom?"

"She approached me."

"I could see that," Pepe said with a grin.

Alessandro blushed.

"And your family?"

"Only child. My parents live in Bergamo."

"What do they do?"

"My mother teaches, and my father is an orthopedic specialist in a small clinic."

"Where did you go to college?"

"What? Is this an interview?"

"No. I'm just curious. I want to get to know you."

"Bocconi."

"Smart, then!"

"I'm not so sure about that."

"And earlier? *Liceo?*"

"A private school in Milan," Alessandro answered. He looked off evasively and seemed sullen. Pepe surmised it was not a good time in Alessandro's life and let the line of questioning drop.

They continued to chat and visit. After lunch, Patrick brought them espressos and sat with them briefly. "Are you guys doing well?"

"Great," Pepe replied. Alessandro nodded.

"What's on the agenda for the afternoon?"

Answering at the same time, they both said, "Read and relax."

"Perfect. Let me know if you need anything."

After wine and a heavy lunch, Alessandro and Pepe both reclined on the lounges and dozed. An hour later, Pepe stirred and peered over at Alessandro. "Could this be the one?" he asked himself quietly. He was smart, distinguished, and thoughtful. They shared common interests, most notably the idea of a family, children, and life in the countryside.

Alessandro must have sensed he was being watched. He opened his eyes and smiled at Pepe. "I must have fallen asleep."

"Me, too. It's so relaxing."

"I'm not getting much work done," Alessandro lamented.

"You deserve a break. I have an idea," Pepe interjected. "Why don't you come to my place for dinner? I can grill a *filetto* or whatever you would like."

"That sounds marvelous."

"Maybe we can watch a movie afterwards."

Alessandro knew more was planned than a movie, but it was a nice pretext. He nodded. "What time?"

"Why don't you come around seven? The light on the ocean is amazing then. We can have a drink on the porch and watch the changing colors."

"Can I bring anything? I could go by the market."

"Just your handsome self."

Pepe, now eager to set things up at home, leaned forward and pivoted on the chaise, slipping on his flip-flops and tee shirt. He stood, gave Alessandro a kiss on his cheek, and said, "See you later."

Alessandro was surprised at Pepe's quick exit, but excited about joining him later.

11

Chapter Eleven – Trial Run

Alessandro pulled up to Pepe's house. He grabbed the bouquet of roses off the front seat and walked to the front door. Pepe had anticipated his arrival and pushed the door open as he stepped onto the porch.

"*Ciao. Benvenuto!*" Pepe said, giving Alessandro a warm embrace and kiss on the mouth.

"For you," he said, handing Pepe the roses.

"*Grazie.* They are beautiful."

Pepe invited Alessandro in. He reached for a vase in the kitchen, filled it with water, and arranged the roses. "Something to drink?"

"Some of your wine would be great."

Pepe poured them each a glass. "Let's go sit on the porch."

They walked outside. As promised, the angled light of the evening had cast a golden sheen on the surface of the sea in the far distance. The hazy horizon had turned a light magenta color. "It's magnificent," Alessandro commented, raising his glass to Pepe's. "*Salute!*" they said in unison.

Pepe studied Alessandro as he took in the landscape. He had tanned over the last couple of days, and his hair had turned lighter. He had on a form-fitting pair of athletic pants and a cotton long-sleeved shirt. Pepe thought he looked terribly appetizing.

Alessandro turned and caught Pepe staring at him. "Well, here we are," Alessandro said, sighing.

"It seems surreal," Pepe noted.

"How so?"

"A few days ago, I noticed you at Nunzia's. An enigmatic guest. Today we are having a quiet evening together as if we were old friends."

"Hmm. Yes. Familiar and yet novel."

"A pleasant surprise."

"Thanks for sharing your world with me. As I mentioned, my grandparents had a vineyard. There's something about the smell of the earth and the solitude of the countryside that is terribly sooth-ing."

"It's funny. A lot of people come to the vineyard and fantasize about a pastoral setting with wine tasting and sumptuous meals. After that, they are bored and find the land isolating."

"As a kid, I loved to explore. I would walk down country roads, discovering streams, groves, and wildlife. I loved the solitude and the chance to think. I always dreamed of having a place like this of my own."

"You're not just saying that?" Pepe asked, incredulous of Alessandro's sentiments.

"No. I'm serious. And it's amazing what you have here – your studio, books, and close family. It must be a terribly rich life."

Pepe stood up and walked over to Alessandro. He leaned down and gave him a protracted, fervent kiss. "No one has ever said that to me before. Where did you come from?"

Alessandro shook his head. He gazed into Pepe's dark, moist eyes. He ran his hand up the back of Pepe's leg. He feared things were moving too quickly – that an unpleasant surprise was lurking around the corner.

Pepe took his hand and lifted him up, leading him inside the house. Inside, he took hold of the back of Alessandro's head and pulled him close, surrounding his lips with his own, breathing him in. "Hmm," Pepe moaned.

Pepe slipped his finger in the folds of Alessandro's collar and massaged his neck. He adroitly moved his hand down and unbuttoned his shirt, sliding his warm hand over Alessandro's smooth chest.

Alessandro's cock firmed up, and Pepe massaged it over the stretchy fabric of his pants. Alessandro reached around the back of Pepe and squeezed his buttocks, pulling him close.

Pepe wanted to throw Alessandro down on the floor and make love to him, but he hoped that might be dessert. "Maybe we should have dinner first!" he suggested.

Alessandro gave him an imploring look. Pepe traced his finger over Alessandro's nose and said, "Later. Right now, I need to feed you. Straighten yourself up," he admonished him, chuckling and pulling the two sides of his shirt together.

Pepe led them into the kitchen. I hope you like beef. I had two nice filets saved for a special occasion. I thought we could grill them. There's a caprese salad, and while the meat is cooking, I can make some risotto."

"What can I do to help?"

Pepe glanced at the kitchen counter and said, "Would you like to make the risotto? Here's some chicken broth and a porcini risotto mix."

"Sounds easy enough." Alessandro pivoted and surveyed the kitchen. The marble counter rested on closed wooden cabinets filled with pots and pans. Above were open shelves, where Pepe had tastefully positioned glasses, cups, and decorative bowls. There was a rustic oak table off to the side, under a window. Colorful ceramics and original art covered the clean, white, wood-paneled walls. A red oriental carpet covered the slate tile floor. "And you wonder why your girlfriends suspected you were gay?" Alessandro said as he gestured at the room and shelves.

Pepe blushed. "Even straight men have an eye for those things."

"Not any that look like you."

"There must be some."

"They are a cocktail away from the other team."

Both laughed, raised their wine glasses, and took a drink.

"Seriously. This is gorgeous," Alessandro said, admiring the room.

"Thanks," Pepe said as he took a platter with two filets on it toward the backdoor. "I'm going to light the grill."

"I'll start the risotto."

Thirty minutes later, they gathered at the kitchen table. Pepe lit some candles, refilled their glasses, and said, "It's so nice to have you here. *Buon appetito!*"

"*Salute!*" Alessandro said, in return, raising his glass to Pepe's. "Hmm," delicious Alessandro said as he took the first bite of the tender filet. "How did you season it?"

"Oil, balsamic vinegar, salt, pepper. Simple. And the risotto is perfect," Pepe added.

Both grew quiet as they ate. They were both deep in thought, imagining where their budding relationship might take them. Was this a ritual to be repeated from time to time – two boyfriends getting together when they could? Or were they rehearsing a daily routine – a life spent together?

Pepe looked up and felt a flutter in his stomach. Alessandro was easy to be with, and conversation flowed. He was handsome and classy. But would the relationship become stale and suffocating with time? Was there enough spark and mystery to keep it going – ten years, twenty years, a lifetime?

Alessandro felt Pepe's regard and glanced up. He smiled contently at the powerful man in front of him – someone who embodied raw male allure yet was tender and soulful. Could he satisfy Pepe, or would he become restless and want something more exotic?

"Do you play any sports?" Pepe inquired.

Alessandro finished a bite of the caprese salad and answered, "In *liceo*, I played soccer. I go to the gym in Milan for cardio and weightlifting. In the winter, I like to ski."

Pepe swallowed hard. Alessandro noticed. "A problem?" he asked.

"I didn't have the best experience skiing."

"Where did you go?

"Vermont."

"Ah. With Patrick and Zeno?"

Pepe nodded. "We went with Massimo. He loves it. Patrick loves it. Zeno tolerates it." Pepe recalled his and Zeno's little escapade one day while back at the lodge. He turned red.

"And you?"

"I've only been a couple of days. I wasn't too good at it."

"I can take you sometime to Courmayeur. I can coach you."

"Hmm. That would be nice," Pepe said, although he hoped he could avoid such an ordeal.

"Do you play soccer or go to the gym?" Alessandro presumed Pepe did something to maintain his physique.

"I have some weights in the basement. I swim at Nunzia's. There's a lot of exercise with work."

"Do Patrick, Zeno, and Massimo go to the States in the winter?"

"Yes. Patrick goes in late August and comes back for the *vendemmia*. Then they all go back after that."

"That must be sad for you."

Pepe sighed. Alessandro seemed exceptionally thoughtful.

"It is. That's why I went with them to Florida last year."

"Will you go this year?"

"Depends on whether I have someone to keep me company here," Pepe said, winking at Alessandro.

"That might be arranged."

"When do you paint?"

"Whenever I have free time. I always have a couple of works in progress."

Alessandro wondered if Pepe needed a certain amount of solitude and how that might work if they got more involved. "Do you have to get into the zone to paint?"

"Not really. I can jump in and spend an hour or two when I have the chance."

"Does it bother you if someone watches while you paint?"

"The situation has never arisen. Why do you ask?"

"Just curious." In fact, Alessandro was already pondering what it might be like for them to share a home – each needing space to work uninterrupted.

They finished their meals. Pepe made them both an espresso. Alessandro helped clear the table. He approached Pepe, who was leaning over the sink. He set the plates down on the counter and reached his arm around Pepe's chest. Pepe pivoted, and Alessandro leaned toward him and gave him a kiss.

Pepe ran his hand along Alessandro's neck. Alessandro pressed himself against Pepe, who started to feel anxious. Alessandro ran his hands up Pepe's thigh and massaged his crotch, reaching for the zipper of his pants. He continued to lean into Pepe, nibbling his ear and whispering, "You're so fucking sexy."

Pepe tried to extract himself, but Alessandro pushed harder, pressing his hard, erect shaft against the bulge in Pepe's pants. Alessandro reached his hands behind Pepe and slipped them into the seat of his jeans, feeling the warm skin underneath. He leaned forward to kiss Pepe, and Pepe gave him a forceful shove. Alessandro fell backwards and hit his head and left eye on a stool.

"*Cazzo! Che fai?* Fuck! What are you doing?" Alessandro screamed as he held his hand against his head.

Pepe froze. He couldn't believe he had lost control. He wanted to apologize, but his body was flush with adrenaline, and he was still in a self-protective mode. He paced back and forth, trying to calm himself.

Alessandro stood and glared at Pepe, waiting for an apology. None was forthcoming. "Maybe I should go."

Pepe shook his head no, but without looking Alessandro in the eye.

Alessandro grabbed his keys and phone. Pepe placed his hand on Alessandro's forearm. "Stay. Let's talk."

Alessandro hesitated. Pepe looked imploringly at him. It was the beginning of an apology.

Pepe placed his hand affectionately on Alessandro's chest and said, "I'll go get some ice. Why don't you sit in the living room?"

Alessandro gave Pepe a tentative sign of acquiescence and walked out of the kitchen. Pepe retrieved the ice, wrapped it in a towel, and came into the living room, where he tenderly pressed it against Alessandro's eye.

"I'm sorry."

"What happened?" Alessandro feared Pepe might not, in fact, be gay.

"I don't know."

"Did I do something wrong? Something you don't like? Something that makes you uncomfortable?"

Pepe didn't answer at first. He continued to apply ice to Alessandro's head, peering furtively into his hazel eyes.

"Are you better now?"

Alessandro replied, "Yes. But what happened?"

"Let me get you a drink." Pepe stood and walked to a credenza, where he poured them each a glass of brandy. He handed one to Alessandro and sat on the adjacent chair.

"Certain things trigger bad memories," Pepe began.

"Ah," Alessandro murmured. "Do you want to talk about it?"

"No. But we should."

"Don't share any more than you are comfortable with."

Pepe's eyes watered. "There was a man at the orphanage. He promised to make me feel better when I wasn't adopted."

"And did you? Feel better?"

"No. Yes."

Alessandro knew all too well the warring sentiments - physical pleasure mixed with pain and discomfort. "Believe it or not, I think I know the conflict."

Pepe furrowed his brow.

"It happened to me, too. An uncle took advantage of my being homesick. My parents sent me to Milan for school. I didn't like the school. My uncle tried to make me feel better. I went into a dark place. So, I understand."

Pepe began to sob. "I'm sorry. I don't know if I can be who you need me to be."

"It's funny. I was afraid my own inhibitions would leave you frustrated or dissatisfied."

"We're fucked."

Alessandro took a long sip of the brandy and looked off across the room. Could things end so precipitously? He was curious, and asked, "How have you dealt with this before?"

"I haven't. If triggered, things have ended. Nothing long term. And you?"

"The same."

"What's your trigger?"

"I'm embarrassed to say."

"We don't have to talk about it."

"You?"

Pepe hesitated. He cleared his throat and said, "Being cornered, being unable to extract myself."

Alessandro was pensive. He slowly formulated words. "It's kind of the same for me. When someone tries to enter - press themself inside - I start to shake."

Pepe recalled having noticed that during their first time together. "So, what do we do?"

"I like you. I wish this could work, but I'm afraid."

"Give me another chance," Pepe implored.

"What if I can't give you what you want?"

"Let's be honest with each other and see how things unfold."

Alessandro nodded. "I'm glad we got this out in the open."

"Me, too."

"Well, I guess I should head back to the inn."

"Why don't you stay?"

"It's not a good idea."

"I don't want to be alone."

"But."

"And you shouldn't drive with your injury," Pepe quickly interjected.

"It's a minor bruise."

"No agenda or pressure. But it would be nice to sleep with you. Hold you."

Alessandro felt his resolve melt. He craved Pepe's body, the power of his arms embracing him. He gave a slight nod.

Pepe smiled. He stood and took Alessandro's hand and led him to the bedroom. "Use the bathroom. There's a fresh toothbrush for you."

Alessandro freshened up and returned to the room. Pepe used the bathroom and came back to find Alessandro already wrapped in the blanket. Pepe slipped off his shorts and slid in. He inched his way to Alessandro's warm body. He nuzzled his firm cock in the folds of Alessandro's buttocks and reached around him, giving him a tender embrace. "*Buonanotte*," he whispered in his ear.

Alessandro placed his hand on Pepe's thigh and pulled him close. "*Sogni d'oro.* Sweet dreams."

12

Chapter Twelve – Bliss

Pepe stirred as the morning sun filtered through the blinds. He and Alessandro had shifted overnight, and Alessandro's back rested against Pepe's chest. Pepe reached his hand around Alessandro's waist and felt his firm sex, stroking it.

Alessandro moaned and arched his back. Pepe nuzzled his nose into the back of Alessandro's head, saying, *"Buongiorno."* He continued to stroke him as he rubbed his own cock against the small of Alessandro's back. "Does this bother you?" he whispered.

"No," Alessandro said. He pivoted and faced Pepe. Their cocks, erect and hard, brushed against each other, sending shivers through their bodies. Alessandro ran his hand over Pepe's brow and then down along his shoulder. "We both carry wounds," he murmured. "Maybe we can find a way to heal them."

Pepe took hold of their shafts and rubbed them together. He gazed at Alessandro, whose muscles flexed as he became increasingly aroused. Alessandro ran his hand along the inside of Pepe's legs and toward his sex, running his fingers around Pepe's balls. Pepe trembled. Pepe let go of their cocks and crawled between Alessandro's legs, running his warm, wet lips around the base of

Alessandro's erection. He wanted to fuck Alessandro, but he now knew that was his trigger. He took hold of Alessandro's shaft and began to glide his hand up and down it, all the while bathing it in hot saliva. Alessandro could hardly contain himself and began to cry, "Oh my God!" He pulled back, and Pepe feared he had grown anxious. But Alessandro opened his legs and helped Pepe reposition himself so that his cock was nestled against Alessandro's and his legs draped around his waist.

Alessandro spit in his hand and took Pepe's cock. Neither felt cornered or trapped, even though their groins were pressed against each other. They savored the intimate contact of their bodies and the feel of each other's hot skin in their hands.

Pepe leaned forward and surrounded Alessandro's lips with his own, his tongue zealously exploring the warm contours of Alessandro's mouth. They closed their eyes and rode the passion of their bodies, seeking consummation and solace.

Alessandro savored the force of Pepe's formidable body – his gliding hand both powerful and tender. He felt safe and desired, enfolded in Pepe's muscular legs. He felt the contours of Pepe's sex in his hand – hard, engorged, and hot.

Pepe squeezed his legs around Alessandro and pressed his heels into his firm buttocks, forcing the two of them closer together. He felt their balls bounce provocatively against each other as they tugged on each other's shafts. Pepe opened his eyes and marveled at the handsome man in front of him, enfolded in him, held by him.

Each relinquished long-held apprehensions and sensed the relief at being able to become vulnerable to another man. Pepe gripped Alessandro forcefully, sliding his hand up and down the hot, moist, supple skin. He ran his fingers over the sensitive end of his sex, and Alessandro exploded in his hand.

Alessandro, in turn, stroked Pepe's sex tightly, feeling it grow thicker. He felt a wave rise from Pepe's groin and traverse his cock. Pepe initially resisted the impending surge and then surrendered to its force, climaxing in a series of vigorous tremors.

They both collapsed into each other's arms, resting their heads on each other's shoulders.

"Whew," Pepe exclaimed, as his breathing returned to normal.

Alessandro remained quiet, and Pepe grew alarmed. He glanced into Alessandro's eyes, only to discover he was crying. He ran his hand over Alessandro's head and asked, "Are you okay? Was that a problem?"

"No. I'm okay. It may be premature, but I feel like I have my body back. I didn't shake. I wanted you in me."

"*Piano, piano.* Let's take our time," Pepe assured him.

"How are you?" Alessandro inquired.

"Happy. Not afraid. I trust you."

Alessandro smiled, then adding levity, he said, "I need coffee!"

"Do I look like the maid?"

"Quite the contrary. But you don't want to have to deal with my *alter ego, Sandrina, senza caffeina.*"

"Let's get you presentable, then," Pepe said, pulling Alessandro out of the bed and throwing his shirt and jeans toward him. Alessandro slipped on his shirt and his undershorts, but left his jeans hanging on the chair.

Pepe strutted naked to the bathroom, cognizant that Alessandro was looking. He found a pair of shorts and flip-flops, put them on, and then walked to the kitchen.

"*Un espresso?*" Pepe asked.

Alessandro nodded. "Can I fix breakfast?"

"What do you have in mind?"

"A frittata or toast or something else?"

"A frittata sounds good. There are eggs, milk, and vegetables in the fridge."

Alessandro opened the door and picked out the things he needed. He reached under the cupboard and found a pan. Pepe gazed at his long, sexy legs as he maneuvered around the kitchen. He handed him an espresso.

Alessandro found it increasingly difficult to temper his obsession with Pepe's sculpted torso as he made coffee, set out plates, and cut up some fruit. "I'll head back to the inn and get out of your way after breakfast."

Pepe paused and gave Alessandro a playful look. "You're not in my way. You can stay, if you like."

Alessandro raised a brow. "I need to work."

"Use my computer."

Alessandro blushed. He realized Pepe wanted him to stay, and he felt embarrassed by Pepe's interest and enthusiasm.

"It will be easier at the inn."

"But then I'll have to drive there later and pick you up."

"For what?"

"A romantic dinner."

Alessandro shook his head in disbelief. "You're amazing."

"Stay. Do your work here. Help me in the field."

"I'm hardly dressed for that."

"I have things you can wear."

"You're persistent."

"Wouldn't you be in you were in my shoes?"

Alessandro approached Pepe and ran his hand along his shoulder. He wanted to press him against the counter and give him a passionate kiss. But he now realized that wouldn't be well-received, and he would have to be careful. They had a lot of work to do healing each other's scars.

"Okay, but I'm taking you out for a romantic dinner tonight."

"We can stay here and cook."

"Let me take you out and show you off."

"Do you have no shame? These are my people around here."

"They need to get used to the new Pepe."

Pepe's eyes widened. Alessandro was definitely putting the moves on him. "Maybe we could go to Ravello?"

"Don't you have an aunt that has a restaurant in the nearby village?"

"I'm not ready for that yet."

"They must know."

"Hmm. I don't think so."

"So, you're not out?"

"Not officially. I think Nunzia knows, at least she's seen enough to put pieces together. My father and mother have no clue."

"Are you sure?"

"I've only dated women."

"Surely Nunzia and they talk."

Pepe furrowed his brow, realizing his façade might not be as seamless as he imagined. "I need to take it slow. I don't want to shock everyone."

"But they are comfortable with Zeno and Patrick, right?"

Pepe nodded.

"Why wouldn't they be accepting of you?"

"I don't know." Pepe realized they would be accepting, but perhaps he wasn't ready to accept himself yet. He gazed at Alessandro and realized there was the real possibility that they might become long-term boyfriends, even partners. The idea excited and frightened him.

Alessandro took Pepe's hand and held it. "This is new for both of us."

"What is? You're out."

"Not to everyone. But that's not what's new."

Pepe gave Alessandro a concerned look. Alessandro hesitated. Slowly, he said, "I like you. I have a feeling this could turn into something. That's scary. What if I'm not enough for you? What if we find differences we can't get past? What will others think - your family and friends and my family and friends?"

Pepe put his finger up against Alessandro's mouth. "Shh." Pepe didn't follow with anything. He looked across the room nervously. He liked Alessandro, too, but the idea of declaring that was terrifying.

Alessandro felt his legs grow weak. Pepe hadn't responded to his sentiments. Had he misread Pepe?

Pepe turned to him, and his eyes were red. "What if I'm not enough for you? What if my life isn't enough?"

"I don't think that's going to be the case."

"I like you, too. Don't hurt me."

Alessandro realized that the powerful and hyper-masculine man in front of him was still a kid who had been terribly disappointed growing up. To make matters worse, he had been mystified as a teen, hearing expressions of affection from grown men who only wanted to take advantage of him. Love had never been authentic or real – it had always been a facsimile. He now appreciated the magnitude of Pepe's trauma, and he feared he wouldn't be able to mend it. "I'll do my best if you will, too."

Pepe smiled. "I'll try."

They kissed. Pepe sniffed the air and then interjected, "I think your frittata might be ready."

"Oh my God, yes!" Alessandro quickly opened the oven door and pulled out the pan. The eggs had turned a beautiful caramel color. "Perfect!" he exclaimed.

"Another coffee?"

Alessandro nodded as he placed the hot pan on a trivet. Pepe reached into a drawer and handed him a serving knife as he pressed buttons on the espresso machine for another coffee. Alessandro cut them each a generous portion, and they both sat down to eat.

"*Buon appetito!*" Pepe said.

"Thank you for welcoming me so warmly."

"I've been waiting a long time for you."

Alessandro smiled contently.

After breakfast, Alessandro did some work on the computer. Pepe checked emails and cleaned the kitchen and bedroom.

"I'm going to go outside to work," Pepe declared as stood near the front door.

"I'll help."

Pepe scrutinized Alessandro, calculating whether he had work clothes that might fit him. "Follow me."

They went into the bedroom, and Pepe rummaged through drawers. He held up a pair of shorts and said, "Try these."

Alessandro held them up to his nose and sniffed them. He raised a brow playfully.

Pepe said, "You're crazy!"

"Sorry!"

Alessandro slipped on the shorts. They fit, although they were a bit loose. He secured them with a belt and then unbuttoned and removed his shirt. Pepe threw him a tee shirt, which he slipped over his head.

"Shoes might be more of a problem," Pepe suggested. Alessandro appeared to have bigger feet.

Alessandro nodded no. He walked to the front of the house and out to his car. In the trunk, he found a pair of running shoes. He held them up triumphantly. Pepe retreated inside and returned with socks. They finished dressing on the front porch, and they strolled into the field.

"We need to trim new growth so that nutrients go to the grapes. And we need to weed around the trunks."

"Easy enough," Alessandro said, as he took a pair of clippers from Pepe.

They began working one of the rows. Pepe said, "So you used to do this with your grandfather?"

"Yes."

"What was he like?"

"A larger-than-life kind of person. Full of energy and excitement."

"What did he do?"

"He was a banker."

"Thus, your interest in finance?"

"Perhaps."

"Did you have cousins?"

"Two males."

"Where are they? Do you get together?"

"Both are in Milan. We get together for holidays. You'll have to meet them sometime."

Pepe felt a twitch in his stomach. Alessandro's comments implied a future and family and holidays. "How are you holding up over there?"

"Fine," Alessandro said, concealing the nagging pain in his lower back.

"We can work a little while longer and take a break."

"Don't let me slow you down."

"Don't worry. I have things to do in the cellar, too. And I need to feed you."

"Don't go to any effort. I can take a break and go back to the inn for lunch."

"And get grilled by Patrick? I don't think so."

"It's adorable – his and Zeno's concern for you."

"They're just looking for the sordid details."

"That's confidential."

"I should hope so," Pepe said. He stood, stretched, and lifted off his shirt. Alessandro's eyes widened at Pepe's profile. Pepe handed him a bottle of water and said, "Here. Drink some water. You need to stay hydrated."

Alessandro took a long sip of water and returned to trimming the vines. He took a deep breath, savoring the aromas of the earth, grass, and the salty breeze blowing up from the sea. He glanced over at Pepe. His heart raced with glee, pondering their growing affection and friendship.

An hour later, Pepe said, "Time to take a break. Let's have a light lunch. Afterwards, I can take care of things in the cellar if you need to work or rest."

"Sounds good," Alessandro said, relieved at the reprieve.

They walked back to the rear of Pepe's house. "There's an outdoor shower and hose if you want to clean up."

Alessandro waited for Pepe to lead. Pepe stripped and turned on the shower. His wet body gleamed in the midday sun. "Come in," Pepe gestured.

Alessandro gave a hesitant look, and Pepe stepped forward and took hold of him, pulling him in under the cascading water. "Let's clean you up," he said.

He unbuttoned Alessandro's shorts, and they fell to the ground. He removed his translucent wet tee shirt and then reached for a bar of soap on a nearby shelf. He began to soap Alessandro's body.

Alessandro instantly grew aroused, and Pepe lathered his hands and began to clean his engorged cock.

Pepe handed Alessandro the bar of soap and turned around. "Can you do my back?"

Alessandro was speechless. He ran his hands over Pepe's muscular back and then down between his buttocks — slick, round, and firm. He ran his fingers deep into Pepe's crack. Pepe turned toward him. He was aroused, too. He opened his mouth and gave Alessandro a kiss, taking hold of Alessandro's sex.

"You are so fucking handsome," Pepe said to Alessandro, who took hold of Pepe's balls and then slid his hand up Pepe's cock.

They stood under the water and stroked each other feverishly. Pepe ran his free hand over Alessandro's slick buttocks while Alessandro nibbled hungrily on Pepe's pecs. Pepe moaned, "Oh my God," as he felt his legs tremble and waves of pleasure course through his body, exploding through his erect shaft. Alessandro watched the spectacle in amazement and then screamed as Pepe gave him one more squeeze, and he came, too.

They clung to each other, waiting for their racing hearts to return to normal. Each took turns letting the water rinse them. Pepe turned off the water and handed Alessandro a towel. Pepe said, "I didn't realize you were going to be such a distraction."

"Sorry. I was just minding my own business."

"You'll have to try harder."

They both chuckled.

"Lunch?" Pepe interjected.

"I think I worked up an appetite."

"I'd say you did."

"Come inside."

Alessandro followed Pepe inside. They went into Pepe's bedroom, where he found something for them both to wear. They returned to the kitchen. Pepe pulled some salad and grilled chicken out of the fridge and prepared them each a plate.

"So, you have some work at the cellar?" Alessandro said, piercing the awkward silence as he ate some of his salad.

Pepe nodded.

"I'll go back to the inn. In can meet you someplace for dinner."

"Why don't you stay? You can work or take a nap. We can go out from here," Pepe suggested, slicing into his chicken breast.

"I should get back."

"Why?"

"Patrick and Nunzia will be worried."

Pepe reached for his phone and dialed Patrick.

"*Pronto*," Patrick said as he picked up the call.

"*Tesoro*, Alessandro is helping me here at the estate. He won't be there for lunch or dinner."

Alessandro grabbed Pepe's phone. "Patrick. This is Alessandro. Sorry I didn't let you and Nunzia know. I'm spending some time with Pepe."

"Not a problem. We figured. Don't let him work you too hard."

"Too late. My back is killing me."

Pepe grabbed the phone back and said to Patrick, "It's not from the hard labor his back is hurting."

Patrick held the phone away from him and stared at it. "Well, well, well," he murmured to himself. Then he said to Pepe, "I'm happy for you. Enjoy! You deserve it."

"Ciao," Pepe said, and hung up.

"Take a break here. We can go out later."

"Should I make reservations?"

"No. I have connections. We'll go to the restaurant in Positano, where Zeno works."

"Sounds perfect."

They finished lunch, and Alessandro took care of the dishes. Pepe walked up the hill to the cellar and did some work.

At seven, they dressed and headed to Positano. Pepe parked the car, and they walked down the hill. Carlo, the maître d', greeted them and showed them a table in Zeno's section. Zeno was taking orders at another table, glanced up, and winked at them.

"Do you come to Positano often?" Alessandro asked Pepe, whose eyes glistened in the sunset's glow.

"Usually just for deliveries."

"I love the setting, here. How often can one sit on the edge of the beach and gaze out at the sea? It's also classy – with table clothes and handsome waiters," Alessandro said as Zeno approached.

"Pepe. Alessandro. What a pleasant surprise!"

"Zeno! Good to see you in your habitat," Pepe said, grabbing his hand affectionately.

"What can I get you to drink?"

"Some of the great Benevento wine?" Alessandro asked.

"*Subito.*" Zeno retreated to the kitchen.

"So, it was here that Patrick made the connection between his grandfather's friend and Zeno?"

"Yes. It all happened here."

"Zeno seems nice."

"He is."

"And is he out as gay here?"

Pepe nodded. "Carlo, the manager, is gay, too." Pepe tilted his head toward him.

"And you and Zeno and Patrick got involved?" Alessandro asked.

Pepe shifted nervously in his chair. He looked off evasively. "Yes, we did."

"How does that work now?"

"What do you mean?"

"Well, you all practically live together – side by side. That must be challenging," Alessandro suggested.

Zeno returned to their table, opened the bottle of wine, and poured them each a glass. Alessandro gazed up at him - at Zeno's wispy lashes, full brows, and deeply set, alluring eyes.

"What can I get for you?" Zeno asked.

"We need to study the menu," Pepe replied.

Zeno rubbed his hand on Pepe's shoulder and said, "Take your time. I'll be back."

"Back to Zeno and Patrick," Alessandro said.

"We're close, and we are family. But we are committed to respecting boundaries."

"Are you ever tempted?" Alessandro pressed. He, in fact, found both Patrick and Zeno very appealing.

Pepe looked off across the restaurant at Zeno. He was tempted. Often. More by Patrick than Zeno. "I came to the conclusion that the more I fought my attraction to them and tried to vilify it as a threat, the more powerful it became. I have grown to accept that they are sexy, but that I have chosen a different path for myself. It is much easier to enjoy the eye candy but stay true to myself."

"Hmm," Alessandro remarked. "That's rather insightful."

"Thank you," Pepe said, grinning.

"No. Really. I find that I spend a lot of energy fretting over desires — resisting them, condemning them, fleeing them. I never considered simply accepting them and then moving past them."

"When I came out to myself, it was very liberating. I didn't realize how big a toll it took to fight my inclinations."

Alessandro lifted his hand and rested his chin on it as if deep in thought. "Maybe that's what Plato was getting at in the Symposium."

"You're going to bring up Plato at a romantic dinner on the beach in Positano?"

"Hear me out."

Pepe sighed and reached over the table, taking Alessandro's hand. "I'm all ears."

"Eros feels irrational and dangerous since it is so powerful and seems to lure us out of our well-structured existence."

"Go on." Pepe said, nodding.

"But eros leads us toward the beautiful and the good."

Pepe yawned.

They both chuckled.

"What do you find appealing about Zeno?" Alessandro asked.

Pepe blushed. "Seriously?"

Alessandro nodded.

"His eyes. They are deep, unfathomable, mysterious."

"What if eros is inviting you to embrace mystery and the boundless horizon of life? Zeno represents something your soul craves and longs for. Yes – he's luscious and delectable. But more importantly, he represents the ocean our souls swim in."

"Isn't that a way of rationalizing away sexual desire?"

"Eros can always lead to its consumption, to its satisfaction. But if that is not prudent, recognizing the graceful side of it can help make the decision easier. It doesn't overlook desire. It integrates it into a soulful response."

Zeno walked up to the table. "Do you guys know what you want?"

Both snickered.

"Sorry," Pepe said. He glanced furtively at the menu and said, "I love the Saltimbocca here. I'll do that and some peas and mashed potatoes."

"And you, Alessandro?"

"The Bronzino with risotto."

"Anything else?"

"Privacy," Pepe said, playfully.

"Back to eros," Alessandro said.

"What about it?"

"It has drawn us together. I find you terribly sexy. It's frightening."

"And what do you make of that, mister philosopher?" Pepe asked.

"I think I needed someone like you to draw me out of myself and away from my comfortable but unhappy life. Your masculinity and physical beauty help me embrace that in myself – that even if I am gay, I am still a man."

"I get that. But there are plenty of other men."

"That's where eros seems to work at another level. Not only are you handsome and fiercely masculine, but there are all these other layers – your art, your philosophy, your thoughtfulness, and your love of the land. And it's amazing that we both have deep traumas that need to be healed. I'm relieved that you understand that."

Pepe took a sip of wine and looked out across the beach. What Alessandro said made sense, but he wrestled with the fact that while Alessandro was handsome, he wasn't exactly his type. How was eros at work in his case?

"I can see how our similar backgrounds are at work here. I appreciate that you understand that about me."

"At the risk of sounding way too serious, what do you want in a relationship?"

"Whew!" Pepe said. "That's a serious question."

"Is it too much?"

"No. But let me take a breath."

"It is too much, isn't it?"

"I'm sitting on one of the most beautiful beaches in the world, across from a handsome man, having a romantic dinner. That's pretty outstanding as it is."

"But?"

"There are no buts." Pepe said, although he continued to wrestle with a nagging hesitancy. "I want someone who can embrace my work and share my life – on the vineyard and amongst my family. Although you live in Milan, you seem to appreciate it here."

"I do."

"I guess I hoped to find someone who was thoughtful, and you are."

Alessandro sighed.

"You know I like art, and I like to read. You share those interests – perhaps even more than I."

Alessandro chuckled. "Too much?"

"No."

Alessandro furrowed his brow. He realized Pepe hadn't mentioned anything physical.

"What's wrong?"

"Nothing."

Pepe sensed Alessandro was apprehensive. He suspected why, and he said, "You're terribly handsome."

The sun had set, and the glow of the candle on the table illuminated Alessandro's face. Patio lights strung overhead caught a few playful tufts of hair on his head. Pepe contemplated the man before him – a tall northern Italian type – classy and blonde. Although he had an impressive frame, his gestures and eyes were warm, tender, and conveyed a sense of vulnerability. Pepe always thought he would have gravitated to someone dark, intense, forceful. Perhaps Alessandro represented something less volatile, a fire that burned slowly – perhaps one that could grow warmer and bolder with time. "Your body is regal, luminous, and resilient. Your eyes are gentle and attentive. I love the feel of your skin against mine and the firmness of your body in my hands."

Alessandro detected Pepe's measured sentiments, but no one had ever said anything similar to him before. He might not be Pepe's type, but Pepe was in touch with his feelings and something deep and long lasting was growing between them.

Zeno came to their table with their dinners. "*Buon appetito*," he said as he set their plates down on the table.

"*Grazie*," both Pepe and Alessandro replied.

Zeno gave them a glance before he left, smiling contently at the evidence of their affection.

After dinner, Pepe and Alessandro strolled through Positano. They stopped at a bar and listened to some live music. They made their way back to Pepe's car and headed down the highway toward Praiano.

"This was an amazing night," Alessandro said. "Thank you."

"Where are you going?"

"You're dropping me off at the inn, right?'

"No. I'm taking you home."

"You're sweet, but I don't want to disturb your routine anymore than I have already."

"I hope my routine might be changing."

Alessandro swallowed hard. There was nothing more he wanted than to crawl into bed with Pepe. "It's been a nice day. Why don't we plan on connecting tomorrow?"

"I want you to stay with me," Pepe pleaded.

Alessandro shook his head no, but his eyes said yes.

They approached the inn. Pepe slowed the car but didn't give any indication he was prepared to stop. Alessandro placed his hand on Pepe's thigh and said, "Let me at least get a change of clothes."

Pepe pulled into the parking lot. He waited in the car while Alessandro went to his room and threw a few things into a small duffle bag. When Alessandro returned, they sped off.

The lights were on at Zeno's and Patrick's house. Pepe quietly pulled the car up to his house and led Alessandro inside. "Shh," he whispered, not wanting to alert Zeno and Patrick to their arrival.

"I'm sure they already know I'm spending the night. My car is here."

"Still. I don't want them to wander over."

"Want a drink?"

"No. I'm exhausted," Alessandro said.

"Me, too," Pepe interjected. He picked up Alessandro's bag and led him into the bedroom. They both used the bathroom, stripped, and slid into bed.

"*Buonanotte*," Pepe said as he reached his arms around Alessandro's torso and pulled him close.

"*Buonanotte*," Alessandro said in reply. Then, almost imperceptibly, he whispered, "*Ti voglio bene.* I love you."

Pepe froze. He felt his heart race, and he wondered if Alessandro could feel it against his back. He was at a crossroads. Might this be the one? Did he need more time? He closed his eyes and sensed a voice in his head – 'go ahead; tell him.'

Pepe squeezed Alessandro and said, "I love you, too. Sweet dreams."

13

Chapter Thirteen – Milan

A month later, Pepe boarded a flight to Milan. He and Alessandro spoke daily, and things continued to progress nicely between them. Alessandro had planned a weekend of activities – sightseeing in the city and a drive to Courmayeur for hiking in the Alps.

At the airport, Pepe exited security with a suitcase in tow. He looked around and spotted Alessandro. He smiled excitedly, walked toward him, and they kissed. "*Ciao, tesoro!* I've missed you so much," Alessandro said, rubbing his hand over Pepe's back.

"Me, too," Pepe replied, grinning from ear to ear.

Alessandro took Pepe's hand and walked with him to the parking garage. Inside the car, in haste, Pepe unbuttoned Alessandro's shirt and slipped his hand inside, massaging his chest. He leaned forward and surrounded Alessandro's lips with his own, breathing him in.

"You feel so good," Alessandro murmured, nibbling Pepe's ear and neck and running his hand along the inside of Pepe's legs.

"*Andiamo?*" Pepe suggested, hoping to get to Alessandro's apartment sooner than later.

Alessandro exited the garage and made his way to the highway. In the distance, Pepe noticed the Alps. "You're so close to the mountains."

"Yes. It's nice. We'll go later in the week."

"How far is the city?"

"Forty-five minutes or an hour. Depending on traffic. You're so tan," Alessandro said, marveling at the contours of Pepe's body just inches from him.

"A lot of outdoor work."

"I hope it's not a problem stealing you away for a vacation."

"Alberto was happy for me."

"So, he knows."

"We had a good talk. And you, how are things going in terms of the divorce?"

"Fine," Alessandro said, concealing some complications. He would save those for later.

"You have some time off?"

"It's August. Offices are either closed or operating on a skeleton crew."

In fact, the highway was deserted, and they were soon in the center. "Wow!" Pepe said as he noticed the spires of the cathedral in the near distance.

"Yes. The Duomo. Our crown jewel."

"I can't wait to see it."

Alessandro maneuvered the dense urban center and pulled up to an apartment complex. "Here we are," he said, pulling into a parking space at the edge of the pavement.

Pepe glanced out of the window. Everything was immaculate — no trash, soot, or graffiti. Alessandro opened the trunk and extracted Pepe's bag. They entered the building and took the small snug elevator to the fifth floor. En route, Alessandro reminded himself not to come onto Pepe. Pepe took several deep breaths and smiled nervously at his chum.

Once inside the apartment, Alessandro pivoted and pulled Pepe to him. He kissed him ravenously. He ran his hands over Pepe's firm chest and breathed in the subtle aromas of the Amalfi Coast and his citrusy cologne. Pepe kissed him back and gazed into his eyes. Each had missed the other, but had grown used to their solitude. Their bodies craved union; their minds urged caution.

"Here we are," Alessandro said, piercing the heavy silence and gesturing toward the expansive interior. Pepe walked to the window and gazed out onto the rooftops of the surrounding buildings. Several skyscrapers loomed in the distance. "Can I get you something to drink?" Alessandro asked.

Pepe nodded. "Perhaps some wine. White."

"Right away," Alessandro said, retreating to the kitchen.

Pepe explored the living room. "I like your art," he remarked disingenuously. It was more abstract and modern than representational.

"I have a new artist I'm hoping to add to the collection," Alessandro said from the kitchen.

Alessandro's space was upscale, modern, and minimalist. Pepe grew nervous. If they began to live together, how would they reconcile their different tastes?

"Have a seat," Alessandro said as he returned with their drinks. Pepe sat on the sofa, and Alessandro joined him. They clinked their glasses and took a sip.

"Is this all new?" Pepe asked, pointing to the furniture and accessories.

"Some of it came from Giada's and my apartment. Her taste is quite different from mine."

Pepe hoped his was more compatible with Pepe's. "How so?"

"Most of this furniture is fit for a torture chamber – it's hard, cold, and uncomfortable."

Pepe chuckled and sighed in relief.

"And how are things going on that front?"

"We can save that for later," Alessandro said. "I want to hear how you are doing."

"I'm fine. The grapes look good. Everyone is healthy and busy. Zeno is in Positano most days. Massimo stays with his grandparents there and Patrick helps Nunzia."

"And you?"

"There's plenty to keep me busy. Deliveries, bottling, and getting ready for the harvest."

"You still want me to come?"

"Of course."

"I won't be in the way?"

"I'm going to put you to work!"

"Like last time."

"Let's put it this way. I would get a trainer to help you build up endurance."

Alessandro gave Pepe a fake frown. "You don't think I'm fit?"

"We'll I'll have to inspect things to answer that."

Alessandro spread his arms wide as if to invite Pepe to begin his work. Pepe's eyes widened with excitement. He leaned forward and unbuttoned Alessandro's shirt. "Hmm, the pecs seem nice and firm." He ran his warm tongue over the smooth surface and added, "And they taste scrumptious."

Alessandro grew aroused. Pepe traced his hand over the bulge in his pants.

Alessandro ran his hand over Pepe's thighs and then traced his finger over his brow. Pepe's eyes were moist with happiness, content to be back in Alessandro's arms. Alessandro reached around

Pepe's shoulder and tugged on his pullover, slipping it over his head. He ran his hand down the center of Pepe's chest to the waist of his jeans and slipped his fingers inside, grazing the hardness of Pepe's erection.

Pepe leaned back, and Alessandro unzipped him. Pepe's large cock sprung free. Alessandro ran his hand along the supple, hot skin. Pepe moaned.

Both were eager to reclaim their companion and savor the taste and feel of each other's bodies. Their conversations had grown lengthier over the past weeks, and they had become increasingly confident in the relationship's unfolding.

Pepe tugged on Alessandro's jeans until they slid down his legs. He reached inside his undershorts and felt his firm, warm cock. He nuzzled his nose in the folds of the fabric, breathing in the scent of his body, one that felt more and more like home. Pepe placed his hands on Alessandro's buttocks and pulled him close. He felt Alessandro's hardness against his face. Forcefully, he pulled Alessandro's undershorts down and surrounded him with his warm, wet lips.

"*Dio mio!*" Alessandro screamed.

"I want to eat you up," Pepe murmured, running his hands up and down the back of Alessandro's legs.

Both felt increasingly safe with each other and let the spontaneity of their desire lead. Alessandro pushed Pepe back onto the sofa and straddled him. He ran his hands voraciously over Pepe's sculpted body — over his firm pecs, his lean abdomen, and his muscular thighs. He took hold of Pepe's sex and stroked it with abandon.

Pepe turned the other direction and edged his way between Alessandro's legs. Alessandro took hold, again, of Pepe's cock, while Pepe licked the back of Alessandro's legs, working his way up his firm, rounded glutes. Alessandro moaned as Pepe's warm, wet lips coated his skin.

Alessandro's thighs grew weak as his body increased in arousal. He rolled to the side and took Pepe in his mouth. Pepe, in turn, ran his lips along Alessandro's hard shaft. Their bodies writhed in each other's arms as they consumed one another without restraint. Each felt as if his body had merged with his companion's. There were no more lines of demarcation of boundaries — just body, breath, and heart.

Pepe let go of all hesitation and felt his body explode in a series of powerful tremors. He felt Alessandro stiffen and come as well, his body shuddering from waves of pleasure that had coursed through him.

Satiated, they rolled onto their backs, clinging to one another on the narrow sofa cushions. When their breathing had returned to normal, Alessandro climbed over Pepe and retrieved his undershorts. He slipped them on and threw Pepe his.

They each reached for their glass of wine and took a long sip. "Whew," Pepe said. "Not bad for a northerner."

Alessandro grinned. He was speechless, mesmerized by the hauntingly handsome man sitting in front of him. He placed his hand on Pepe's knee and said, "I'm glad you are here."

The light outside had changed as the sun set. Alessandro stood, turned on a few lamps, and went to the bathroom. When he came out, Pepe was examining photographs on the credenza.

"Are these your parents?" Pepe inquired.

Alessandro walked up behind him and said, "Yes. Last summer. In Bergamo."

"You have your father's distinguished profile and your mother's eyes."

"Hmm," Alessandro murmured.

Pepe realized Alessandro would age well, as his father had. "And who are these?"

"My cousins, aunts, uncles, parents, and Giada."

Pepe lifted the photograph closer and focused on Alessandro's wife. "She's beautiful."

"And a princess. Very high maintenance."

"Do you miss her?"

Alessandro felt his chest twitch. He shook his head no. "Shall we take a walk and go to dinner?"

"Sounds great. Let me change."

Pepe went to the bedroom and put on dressier clothes. Patrick had accompanied him on a trip to Naples to pick out things for his visit to Milan, a decidedly more fashionable city. Alessandro came in and said, "*Bello!*"

"*Troppo* – too much?"

"No, but the girls will be salivating."

"What are you going to wear?"

Alessandro held up a summer shirt and some slacks. "It's August and a bit more casual."

Alessandro dressed and Pepe ran his fingers through his hair, gazing at the mirror.

They went outside and walked to the Duomo, lit up with spotlights. They stood in the expansive pedestrian area and gazed up at the towering church.

"It's amazing," Pepe noted. "I've never seen anything with so much detail — all the spires and statues on the façade."

"The façade was completed several hundred years after craftsmen first began the project. The building was begun in the 14th century after the earlier basilica was destroyed by fire. The first church on the site was built in the 4th century, and its baptistry can be visited in the excavations underneath. Aside from St. Peter's, it is the largest church in Italy."

"Can we go in?"

"It's closed now. We'll visit it later in the week, when we will walk along the roof."

Pepe's stomach fluttered. He didn't like heights.

They continued to walk through the historic center, aglow in streetlights. Alessandro led them to a trattoria, and they walked inside. It was an elegant place with an arched brick ceiling and plaster walls filled with beautiful black and white photographs of Milan. "This is one of my favorite places," Alessandro beamed as he waved to one of the waiters.

"Alessandro! It's good to see you. Welcome. Table for two?"

Alessandro nodded, and they sat.

The waiter leaned over the table and set out water and gave them menus. "How's Giada?" he asked.

"Fine," Alessandro replied, trying to avoid Pepe's eyes.

"To drink?"

"*Un Nebbiolo di Langhe, per favore.*"

The waiter retreated to the cellar and returned with a bottle of red wine. He opened it and poured each a glass.

Alessandro swirled the wine in his glass and lifted it to Pepe's. Pepe forced a smile, worried that perhaps this was Alessandro's and Giada's regular place. He said, "*Salute.*"

"Everything is excellent here," Alessandro said quickly, hoping to distract Pepe.

"Do you and Giada come here often?" Pepe asked, matter-of-factly.

"We did. We haven't since negotiations began about the divorce."

"Ah," Pepe said, relieved.

Alessandro smiled warmly at him and sighed. "I'm so happy you are here."

"Me, too," Pepe replied with a grin.

"The Osso Buco is phenomenal here."

"Maybe I'll try that. I need to get used to northern cuisine."

"Yes. I am glad you are open to the idea of spending some time here."

"And you, down south."

Alessandro nodded excitedly. "I can work from either place. You know how I love the Amalfi Coast and the vineyard. I just hope you won't find Milan too cold or stuffy."

"It's nice to get away in the winter. It's quiet there, and I don't have that much work."

The waiter came, and they ordered. Alessandro grew increasingly edgy, fidgeting with his napkin, drinking a lot of wine, and looking across the room.

"What's up?" Pepe asked.

Alessandro cleared his throat. "There's been a little development."

Pepe felt blood rush to his face. "What kind?" He feared Alessandro and Giada were having second thoughts about the divorce.

"I don't know how to frame this, so I'm just going to blurt it out. Giada is pregnant."

"What? The one who didn't want children?"

"Yes, it's ironic."

Pepe was surprised at the swiftness of the question that flowed off his tongue. "Is it yours?"

"Probably not."

"What do you mean, probably not?"

"The timing is uncertain. As I mentioned before, once I came out, she started having affairs."

"So, it's not yours."

"It could be. We had sex once in June."

"But she's had sex with countless other guys, right?"

"She's been downplaying that lately."

"To pin this on you?"

"Yes. That would be her way to get back at me."

"Is she going to have it?"

"She and her parents are very conservative. Abortion is not an option."

"What about raising it as a single mother?"

Alessandro shifted nervously in his chair. He took a long sip of wine and said, "That's where there's a little problem. She and her parents don't want the child to be illegitimate. At least until it is born, she is not going to agree to a divorce."

"What about after its birth?"

"That's uncertain."

"Where does that leave you? Us?"

"We need to talk."

"Most definitely," Pepe said, his heart racing agitatedly.

"I'm trying to figure things out. We just found out," Alessandro began.

Pepe grew angry at the term, we. The 'we' excluded him, or at least made him feel like an appendage in the negotiations.

"And?"

"I don't know. I love you, and I don't want to mess this up."

"But?"

"I've always wanted to have children."

"Maybe now you can," Pepe said pointedly, glaring at Alessandro.

The waiter arrived with their dinners. Alessandro lifted his knife and fork and began to cut into the tender veal. Pepe pushed his plate to the side and stared at Alessandro.

"Until recently, as a single man or as a gay couple, I couldn't or we couldn't adopt a child in Italy. Even with the new laws, it's uncertain if I or we would be approved."

"Zeno and Patrick were able to do so."

"It's rare."

"So, let me understand. You and Giada would remain married until the baby is born. Then what? Would you get a divorce with joint custody or would you raise it yourself?"

"That's what I wanted to talk with you about. But this doesn't seem to be going well."

"No. It isn't," Pepe said. He took a sip of wine and continued to ignore his dinner.

"Giada doesn't know what to do. She never wanted kids, but now she's having second thoughts."

"So, it's more likely she would ask for joint custody."

Alessandro nodded reluctantly.

"And does she know about me?"

"Yes."

"How is that going to go over? She could easily convince a conservative judge to award her sole custody. You remain married so that the baby is legitimate and then get screwed in the end."

"But there's a chance she would not want to raise the child at all. In that case, I would get custody. And, if you haven't dumped me by then, we could raise the child together."

As much as Pepe wanted children and a husband, the scenario had catastrophe written all over it. "In the meantime, I'm the lover on the sidelines, hanging around to see what happens."

Alessandro set down his knife and fork and buried his face in his hands. He began to sob uncontrollably. "I'm fucked. I'm so sorry."

Pepe was moved by Alessandro's anguish, but he wasn't ready to let him off the hook. He simply watched as Alessandro slowly recomposed himself, then he said, "Please forgive me, Alessandro. I know this can't be easy, but I can't go along with this. I've worked too hard and given up too much to agree to be a lover on the side or someone who would raise your child jointly with your ex-wife."

"I understand."

"I'm not sure you do. Why did you invite me here?"

Alessandro shook his head. He realized he had miscalculated Pepe's reaction. "I guess I had hoped we might figure this out together."

"It's not for me to figure out. You and Giada have to."

"But I need you."

"This has to be more than your needing me. Love means embracing the other person and honoring who they are and the values that are important to them."

"I do."

"No, you don't. I am an orphan, and I will no longer tolerate being considered an adjunct or second-class member of a family."

"You aren't."

"I am if you are still married to Giada or if a child we bring into our relationship belongs to her, too."

"I thought of all people you might understand, be able to embrace a child who has a complicated status."

Pepe stood and dropped his napkin angrily on the table. He walked out of the restaurant. Alessandro followed him.

Outside, Alessandro ran to Pepe and took hold of his elbow and said, "Pepe. Please, let's not end on this note. I am a mess, and I am confused."

"Well, when you have more clarity, let's talk."

"*Tesoro*, please. I need your help. I'm sorry if I hurt you."

"I need some space. We can talk later."

"Where are you going?"

"To find a hotel room."

"Don't. Come back to my place. I'll sleep on the sofa."

"No. We'll talk later." Pepe walked off.

Pepe wandered through the center of Milan and found a small hotel with a vacancy. He booked a room and called Patrick.

"*Pronto, Pepe*," Patrick replied when he saw the call. "How's Milan?"

"Terrible."

"What happened?"

"Giada is pregnant. Alessandro is conflicted."

"Oh, Pepe. I'm so sorry. What devastating news. Why don't you fly home?"

"I have a hotel room tonight. I'll see how I feel tomorrow."

"What did Alessandro propose?"

"Until the baby is born, he would remain married, although we would be together."

"And after the birth?"

"It depends on her. If she wants to raise the child, there might be joint custody."

"Is it his baby?"

"They don't know."

"What are you going to do?"

"You know my position on all of this. I want a husband who is not involved with someone else. If we have children, which I would like, I don't want to be raising them with an ex."

"Then stick to your plan."

"But I love him."

"Don't compromise on who you are to suit someone else's predicament."

"But this is the closest I have come to finding someone who is compatible and who finds my life agreeable, even desirable."

"Stick to your vision. If he loves you, he will come around."

"I don't think so. Giada's family seems to be quite persuasive. I think he will cave."

"Why don't you fly home?"

"We'll see. Thanks for talking. I needed to hear your voice."

"Call anytime. I love you."

"I love you and Zeno, too."

"*Ciao. Buonanotte*," Patrick concluded.

Pepe turned off his phone so he wouldn't keep seeing Alessandro's texts. The next morning, he had breakfast and took a long walk. The prior evening seemed like a nightmare, and he wished it had only been a dream. It wasn't. He concluded that Alessandro and Giada would have to work things out on their own.

He opened his phone and composed a text. "Alessandro. I'm going to fly back to Naples. You have to work this out yourself. I'll come by and get my suitcase."

Alessandro replied. "Please stay. We can work this out — you and I."

"I can't."

"Please."

"I have a flight later," Pepe texted, although he didn't.

"Have lunch with me."

Pepe paused. He didn't want to see Alessandro. But he realized leaving things up in the air wasn't good, either. He typed and then stopped and then continued, "Okay."

"Come to the apartment, and we will walk from there."

"See you," Pepe finished.

Pepe and Alessandro met at Alessandro's apartment and walked to a nearby trattoria. Neither said anything en route. They got a table, ordered drinks, and faced each other.

"I'm sorry," Alessandro began.

"I know. But it's not enough."

"Be patient while I work this out."

Pepe shook his head no. But Alessandro was saying the right things. He was taking responsibility and asking for time. Pepe knew he should agree, but he was angry and hurt.

"I've come too far to compromise."

"I'm not asking you to."

The waiter came to their table and took orders. Pepe took a long sip of wine and looked off across the restaurant. He couldn't look Alessandro in the eyes. He was too handsome and being too solicitous. Pepe knew his resolve was weakening.

"I have to work this out, and I promise I will," Alessandro continued.

"If you wanted to, you would have already."

"I just found out. We were supposed to sign papers two weeks ago, and then she sprung the news."

"Is she trying to get back together with you?"

"I don't think so. She doesn't like me all that much. But it's all about appearances. As long as the baby is born while we are married, she saves face."

"Are you going to keep your own apartment?"

"Yes. I can't live with her."

Pepe murmured under his breath, "That's a relief." Out loud, he asked, "When is the baby due?"

"Sometime in March."

"That's a long time from now. A lot could happen."

"I know. It's unfair for you to put your life on hold."

Pepe wrung his hands. The waiter came with their lunches. Pepe was hungry and dipped a fork into the steaming bowl of rigatoni with sausage and cream. Alessandro watched, trying to detect evidence of Pepe's disposition. He then began to eat his lasagna.

Pepe paused. He looked up at Alessandro and asked, "What if you refuse her demands?"

"What do you mean?"

"Can you divorce her unilaterally?"

"Not in Italy."

"Could you refuse her joint custody?"

"She would win. I'm gay."

"So, there's not much you can do?"

"The only thing I can do is deny paternity or refuse joint custody, although I would probably have to pay child support."

Pepe began to appreciate the gravity of Alessandro's predicament. He took a few bites of pasta and chewed it pensively, turning several scenarios over in his head. None of them looked promising – except one – where Giada gave birth, signed divorce papers, and gave custody to Alessandro. That seemed unlikely. He wondered if it was best to cut his losses and move on.

There was a protracted moment of silence and then Alessandro said, "Change of subject. How's your art?"

"Hmm. Good. I've been working on some new pieces." He had been working on one for Alessandro, a gift for his apartment. He decided not to mention it.

"Are you reading anything new?"

"*Separate Rooms*, by Tondelli."

"I don't know it."

"Story of a gay guy whose lover dies. It's a deep philosophical and interior reflection of his life, his loves, his experiences."

Alessandro blushed. He realized the plot might not be that removed from Pepe's future. "Anything lighter? A beach read?"

"Some books by Philippe Besson, although they are rather serious, too. And you? Still reading Plato?"

"I'm not reading anything at the moment. I'm too preoccupied."

"What about friends?"

"What about them?"

"Do you have friends you can hang out with and get some advice?"

"The friends Giada and I have, have sided with her. I haven't made many friends in the gay community yet."

"Do you go out? To bars?"

"Not really. It's August and most are quiet. Plus, I was never into the gay scene."

Pepe found that reassuring. He wanted a partner who enjoyed quiet evenings at home, watching a movie, or getting together with family.

"What do you do for fun?"

"Work."

"I always heard that about northern Italians, but I never believed it."

"A little levity from our southerner?"

"Don't get used to it. I'm still angry."

"I get it. I hope you are more disappointed than angry. I didn't create the problem."

"I realize that. I guess I'm frustrated that there aren't any good solutions. And I wish you would have told me before I bought new clothes and a ticket to Milan."

"You would have never come."

"Probably not."

"I have an idea. Why don't we drive to Courmayeur?"

"When? Today?"

"Yes. It's only two-and-a-half hours away."

"I thought we were going to spend time here and do that later."

"I need to take a ride, clear my head, walk in the fresh air. I would love for you to accompany me."

Pepe looked over at his phone resting on the table. He stared at it as if it held a response. "Well."

"Is that a yes?" Alessandro interjected excitedly.

"Not yet. I need some time to consider it."

"Can you cancel your flight?"

"I don't have one."

"You've been playing me all along?"

"No. I was going to go back. I'm terribly angry."

"Me, too. A hike in the Alps will do us both good."

"And you have a place there?"

Alessandro nodded. "In fact, it's mine, not Giada's and mine. I wanted to clear out her things. It might be cathartic."

"Where's your grandfather's vineyard? Is it on the way?"

"It's no longer in the family."

"But you know where it is, right?"

"I think I could reconstruct the route in my head."

"I'd like to see it."

Alessandro glanced at his watch and said, "If we leave soon, we could stop in the wine region and then still make it to Courmayeur for dinner."

Pepe placed his finger on his lips, as if deep in thought. He hesitated, creating a dramatic effect. He could tell Alessandro was nervous. He wasn't ready to let him off the hook yet, but he was not as worked up as he was before. "I'm up for a drive, if you are."

"Nothing would make me happier."

"Eat up!" Pepe commanded him.

Alessandro quickly consumed a few more bites of his lunch, waved down the water, paid the bill, and stood, gesturing for Pepe to follow.

14

Chapter Fourteen – The Alps

Pepe rose the next morning to use the bathroom. They had arrived late the night before, having stopped in Langhe to see Alessandro's grandfather's former property nearby. They had dinner at a nice country estate and continued the journey to Courmayeur.

Pepe peeked out of the bathroom window and exclaimed, "*Cazzo!*"

Alessandro stirred and ran to the bathroom. "What's wrong?"

"Nothing. Look!"

"Yes, it's magnificent. It's Mont Blanc – or Monte Bianco, as we call it on the Italian side," Alessandro said, running his hand along Pepe's lower back.

"It's right in your face," Pepe said, referring to the massive peaks towering in front of them.

"My parents used to ski, and they bought the chalet years ago. We are close to the town center. But here on the periphery, there's nothing obstructing the views."

Pepe's heart raced as he contemplated the massive range bathed in morning light. "And you ski up there?"

"No." Alessandro took Pepe's hand and led him to a large window in the living room. "That's where we ski," he said, pointing to a lower group of slopes.

"They are still intimidating," Pepe said.

"At the risk of sounding corny, you are the intimidating one," Alessandro said, pivoting toward Pepe and tracing his hand over Pepe's nude body.

Alessandro leaned forward as if he were about to give Pepe an embrace. Pepe put his hand on Alessandro's chest and said, "Not before coffee."

"Can I get dressed first?" Alessandro inquired.

"I kind of like you like this."

"At least a pair of shorts?" Alessandro retreated to the bedroom, picked up their undershorts and brought them into the living room. He tossed a pair to Pepe. "Get presentable."

They went into the kitchen, where Alessandro turned on the espresso machine and searched the freezer for croissants. Pepe's gaze was glued to the landscape outside, although from time to time he gave Alessandro a scrutinizing look. He continued to grow on him - his smooth lean chest, the curvature of his back, his long powerful legs, and his solicitous hazel eyes.

Alessandro slid a cup of espresso to Pepe and began to bake several croissants. "How did you sleep?"

"I crashed. How much wine did we drink?" Pepe asked, rubbing his head.

"Enough that you slept from Torino to here."

"And how did I end up undressed?"

"That was easy," Alessandro remarked, raising a brow playfully.

"You're still on probation," Pepe noted, realizing a lot of complications still lurked in the air.

"I realize that. I'm appreciative that you haven't cast me off yet."

Pepe stood and walked to Alessandro. He reached his arms around him and gave him a tender hug. "I'm sorry you are going through this, and I have to admit, I'm disappointed and sad. But maybe we can figure things out."

"I would like that."

They enjoyed breakfast, showered, and found suitable hiking clothes and shoes in the closet. They drove to the nearby Dolonne parking area and then took the gondola up to Plan Chéchrouit, where they embarked on a hike along trails overlooking the glacier-studded peaks of the Mont Blanc range.

"You ski these slopes?" Pepe inquired, pondering the steep terrain.

Alessandro nodded. "They aren't as difficult as they look."

"It is rather stunning – the forests, the undulation of the land, and the glaciers in the distance. I've never seen anything like it."

"It's the highest peak in Europe. On busy weekends in the winter, the place is packed with people from Milan."

"Does Giada ski?"

"She has mastered the lodge scene."

Pepe blushed. He had, too, and memories of Lorenzo back in Stowe flashed before him. In retrospect, he was back where he started, falling for a married man. He grew quiet and pensive.

They walked for another kilometer in silence, listening to the rustling wind blowing through the fir trees and the cries of an occasional hawk soaring toward its prey on the grassy meadows. "Are you okay?" Alessandro finally asked, concerned about Pepe's reserve.

"Just thinking."

"Do you mind sharing?"

"I don't see how this is going to work out, sorry to say," Pepe began.

Alessandro turned to him and furrowed his brow.

Pepe continued. "I don't want to stand between you and your desire to have kids. I can't see you walking away from the baby, even if the paternity is in question. And I don't want to raise a child jointly with you and Giada."

They walked forward in silence. Alessandro stared at the gravel path before them. He slowly said, "Does that leave us at an impasse?"

"The only thing that might break it is if Giada doesn't want anything to do with the baby, and that's unlikely, even for someone who doesn't want children."

Alessandro realized Pepe was probably right, and he felt a pit in his stomach. "Can you give me time?"

"How much?"

"This is still new, and Giada's thoughts are all over the place. Maybe things will work themselves out sooner than later."

Pepe didn't respond. They continued to walk, both deep in thought.

Alessandro broke the silence. "There's a restaurant down there." He pointed to a building nestled on a ridge overlooking a stream. "Lunch?"

"Sure," Pepe said.

They carefully made their way down the steep incline and rocky path. Once they arrived at the establishment, the maître d' showed them a nice table, and they ordered drinks.

"I'm so thirsty," Pepe said.

"Since we are high in elevation, the air is dry. Plus, you walked our asses off. I'm not used to so much exercise."

"I thought you went to the gym," Pepe said, nudging Alessandro's shoulder playfully.

"It's easier there. No inclines."

"What's good to eat here?"

"They have a special stew made of mountain goats as well as regional pasta options," Alessandro said.

"This looks good," Pepe said, placing his finger on the menu. "Rigatoni with sausage and a creamy herb sauce."

"Hmm. Yes. But I think I will get the stew."

The waiter came and took their orders.

"This is nice," Alessandro said, peering into Pepe's eyes. "I'm glad you came here with me."

Pepe blushed. He liked the attention Alessandro was paying him, but he was still annoyed at the complicated situation Alessandro was in with Giada. "You're very handsome," Pepe said, out of the blue. The mountain light had brightened his hair, and his eyes glistened.

"So, we're okay?" Alessandro asked, mistaking Pepe's compliment for a truce.

"Not exactly. You and Giada still have a lot to work out. We'll have to see what happens in the meantime."

Alessandro had a worried look on his face. He realized Pepe wouldn't hang around indefinitely.

The waiter came with their lunches. Both took a sip of wine and began to eat.

"Hmm," Pepe said. "This is delicious."

"A local family runs the place. They have a devoted following. In the winter, you can ski down here and have lunch – even sitting outside when the sun is out."

"It must be nice."

"You'll have to come ski with me."

"I'm not sure about that. It wasn't a good experience when I skied in Vermont." What Pepe didn't want to say was that he worried they wouldn't be together in the winter. He sensed Giada would be hard to shake.

They continued to eat, visit, and enjoy the scenery. After lunch, they retraced their steps and boarded the gondola that would bring them back to town. Halfway down the mountain, Alessandro got a call. Pepe could hear a woman hysterical on the other end of the line. He assumed it was Giada. When the call ended, Alessandro looked up.

"That was Giada."

"I assumed."

"She's in the hospital with some complications. She's freaking out over the pregnancy, her health, and our situation."

Pepe felt blood rush to his face. He knew what this meant.

"I'm afraid I need to go see her. We need to head back to Milan right away."

"I understand," Pepe said, but he didn't. Alessandro seemed to cave rather easily.

"I'm sorry. Her parents are away traveling, and she doesn't have anyone around."

"What about one of her boyfriends?"

"I have to be there," Alessandro said matter-of-factly.

The gondola arrived at its base terminus, and they got out of the cabin and made their way to Alessandro's car. They drove back to the chalet, packed, and sped off toward Milan.

"Why don't you drop me off at the airport?" Pepe said.

"You can stay. I just need to make sure she's okay at the hospital. You can hang at my place. I'll be there later."

"I don't want to be in your way."

"You're not."

"I am. Plus, I don't want to be hanging around waiting for you."

Pepe's sentiments frightened Alessandro. It was as if Pepe was saying much more – that he didn't want to wait around for Alessandro. He was moving on.

Both grew quiet. Alessandro was worried about Giada and the baby, unable to talk. Pepe sat brooding over the untenable situation. As they got closer to Milan, both wished they could surmount their pride and say something; neither did.

"The airport is just ahead," Alessandro finally said.

"Just let me off at the curb," Pepe added.

"Do you have a flight?"

"I'll deal with that when I get inside."

"I'm so sorry," Alessandro said.

"Me, too. I like you."

"I'll fix this."

Pepe didn't reply. He wasn't convinced. His silence said much, and Alessandro felt a pit in his stomach. They pulled up to the departure area of the airport, and Alessandro parked the car and got out. Pepe reached into the trunk and retrieved his suitcase. He leaned into Alessandro and gave him an embrace and a kiss on his cheek. "*Ciao*."

"*Ciao*," Alessandro said in reply.

Neither said, 'see you later,' or 'I'll call,' or 'I love you.' Pepe walked away without looking back. It was one of the most difficult things he had ever done.

15

Chapter Fifteen – The
Harvest

A month later, Pepe stacked baskets at the edge of the vineyard
in preparation for the first day of the *vendemmia*. Massimo
followed him, setting out boxes of clippers.

"Do we have enough?" Pepe asked his young assistant.

"How many are coming tomorrow?" Massimo asked.

"Around twenty."

"Then we have enough," Massimo said proudly as he counted
the tools with his fingers.

"What's the weather going to be tomorrow?" Pepe asked. He already knew, but wanted to elicit Massimo's help.

"I don't know," Massimo said. He glanced up at the sky and
said, "It looks like it will be good."

"Can you check on your tablet and see what the forecast says?"

Massimo nodded and ran into his house. He came outside,
launched the weather app, and read the forecast. "Sunny and
warm."

"We'll need to make sure there is enough water for the workers."

Massimo glanced toward Pepe's truck, where cases of bottled water had been loaded. "*Ci penso Io*," Massimo said, conveying that he would take charge of that.

"*Grazie*. It will be a busy day tomorrow. Are your dads going to help?"

"Yes. Both."

"Perfect."

"Do you want to have dinner with us this evening? Papa is making pizza."

"Wow! Pizza! That would be fantastic," Pepe said, tapping into Massimo's enthusiasm and warm hospitality.

"Why don't you ask your papa and make sure it is okay?"

Massimo ran into the house.

"Papa, can *Zio* Pepe have pizza with us tonight?"

"I'm sure he's busy," Zeno replied.

Massimo took Zeno's hand and dragged him to the front porch. "He said he would like to come," Massimo said, gesturing to Pepe.

"So, you already invited him?"

Massimo nodded.

"Then, he's welcome," Zeno said, winking at Pepe. "Don't you have some homework?" Zeno asked his son.

Massimo looked sadly at the ground. "*Si*," he said.

"Why don't you do your work, and I will visit with *Zio* Pepe?"

Regretfully, Massimo went back into the house and began his homework. Zeno waved to Pepe and said, "Do you want some coffee?"

Pepe nodded. "Let me clean up, and I'll be over." Pepe went to the back of his house, stripped, and showered. He put on a fresh tee shirt and shorts and returned to Zeno's and Patrick's house. Zeno saw him coming and prepared an espresso.

"Here you go," Zeno said, handing him a small cup of frothy dark coffee.

"Thank you."

"Is everything ready for tomorrow?"

"Yes. Massimo has been a help."

"He's not in the way?"

"No. It's fun to give him responsibility and watch him rise to the occasion. Alberto did the same for me."

"We're so lucky that you take such an interest in him."

"I enjoy it. I wish I had a son I could raise as well."

"Maybe you will. Have you heard any more from Alessandro?"

"I'm afraid I haven't encouraged him much. We didn't leave off well when I returned from Milan. We text once in a while, but he's still taking an active role in Giada's pregnancy. I've made it clear that I am not interested in co-parenting with her."

Zeno pivoted and busied himself with some things on the kitchen counter. He and Patrick believed Pepe needed to be more flexible. No situation was perfect. At least he and Alessandro were well-matched and could be parents, even if in conjunction with Giada.

"Can you slice the cheese and mushrooms and peppers for the pizza?" Zeno asked.

Pepe nodded and pulled out a cutting board. He rummaged through the fridge and pulled out things for the pizza toppings. He began to slice them. Zeno needed something in the cupboard above him and reached around his shoulder. Pepe breathed in the familiar scents of Zeno's body – a mélange of the soap he used, a bit of cologne, and salty sea air that rose from the coast and blew across the vines. As he reached up, Zeno grazed his shoulder, and

Pepe felt goosebumps race across his back. To brace himself, Zeno placed a hand on Pepe's shoulder. Pepe wanted to turn and give Zeno an embrace. He longed for his and Patrick's bodies and wondered if he needed to rethink things. Maybe the three of them were a better option than waiting for mister right.

Pepe and Zeno prepared the pizzas. Massimo did his schoolwork. And Patrick eventually arrived after a long day at Nunzia's inn.

Surprised to see Pepe, Patrick said, "*Ciao, bello!* Is everything ready for tomorrow?"

"Yes. We're all set. Are you?"

"I need a drink," Patrick said, chuckling.

Zeno poured him a glass of wine and handed it to him. "How was work?"

"Not bad. September is slower."

"You have tomorrow off."

"I do at Nunzia's, but not here."

"I'll take it easy on you," Pepe said.

"Where's Massimo?"

"Doing schoolwork, although it is very quiet back there. I wonder if he fell asleep."

"He's been helping me all afternoon," Pepe interjected.

Patrick walked back to Massimo's room. He had, indeed, dozed off. Patrick sat on the edge of his bed and ran his hand over his playful, dark hair. "*Ciao, figlio.* Are you ready for some pizza?"

Massimo stirred, rubbed his eyes with the back of his hands, and nodded, sliding off the side of the bed and walking briskly to the kitchen. Patrick followed him.

Everyone sat at the kitchen table while Zeno slid a large pizza onto the pizza stone in the oven. Soon, it was ready. He sliced it and gave everyone a piece, sliding a second pizza into the oven.

"Pepe, have you heard from Alessandro?" Patrick asked.

"We were just talking about that," Zeno noted.

"And?"

"Just a text here and there. Nothing has changed," Pepe said.

"How's Giada?"

"Her health is fine, and the pregnancy seems to be progressing well."

"Are they living together?"

"No," Pepe said, slicing a bit of pizza and putting it into his mouth.

"Have you gone on any other dates?" Zeno asked.

Pepe glanced at Massimo. He raised a brow as if to suggest yes.

"Details?" Patrick asked.

"Not at the table," Pepe replied. "Later."

"Anything promising?"

"No. People don't seem interested in vintners."

"They don't know what they are missing," Zeno said, winking at Pepe.

"It's the same. Some good exchanges on the app, a drink, a few extracurricular activities, then *basta*. No interest in long-term relationships or, if they are, not with someone who lives in a remote village on a farm."

"*Pazienza*," Patrick said. "It will happen when it is supposed to."

"Said by someone for whom it has all worked out."

"It will," Patrick added.

"We'll see."

They continued to eat, drink, chat, and then enjoyed a coffee and some dessert. Zeno put Massimo to bed, and Pepe excused himself. "It's going to be a busy day tomorrow. I should go."

Zeno and Patrick glanced at each other. They would have liked Pepe to remain, to join them on the sofa for a movie. "We understand," Zeno said.

Pepe gave Zeno and Patrick kisses and headed out the door.

The next morning, at dawn, cars began arriving at the vineyard. Paolo had set up a small table with coffee and croissants. Massimo had an early breakfast and joined Pepe at the edge of the vines, where he helped assign workers to specific rows.

Zeno and Patrick worked together, keeping a close eye on Massimo from a distance. Despite the tiring work, Patrick treasured all that the harvest signified. There was something magical about standing in a field overlooking the coast, and clipping bunches of ripe grapes. The view was surreal – the cascading mountains, the dark blue water, the terraced houses, and the brilliant clear sky. The smell of the earth and the feel of grass under his feet were like a soothing tonic. Patrick savored the sounds surrounding him — the local dialect, traditional folk songs, and the chirping of birds, hoping to swoop in on insects disturbed by all the commotion.

Alberto observed from the top of the vineyard. As the day progressed and the heat intensified, he decided to break early and serve lunch. He called Laura and Paolo, who soon arrived in their van with tables, cloths, platters of food, and carafes of wine and water. People rinsed off, changed shirts, and gathered to eat.

Pepe didn't join the workers for lunch. He wasn't in the mood to celebrate or socialize. Earlier in the summer, he had looked forward to having Alessandro join in the festivities of the harvest. His absence, while expected since they hardly spoke, punctuated the reality of their distance.

Pepe loaded the last basket into the trailer and drove it up the hill to the cellar. He began to dump the grapes onto the conveyer belt that led to the crusher.

Alberto and Massimo appeared at the cellar after lunch.

"Do you need any help?" Alberto asked.

"No. I'm almost finished."

"How do things look?" Alberto continued.

"Good. Right, Massimo?" Pepe replied.

Massimo nodded. "The sugar content is excellent," he added.

Alberto and Pepe laughed.

"If you need to go home, I can watch Massimo and walk him home later," Pepe said to his father.

"Is that okay with you?" Alberto inquired of Massimo.

Massimo jumped with excitement. He loved helping Pepe.

Alberto left, and Massimo and Pepe finished loading the grapes, completing the first crush. They walked down the hill. Zeno and Patrick were sitting on their porch with someone. It wasn't clear who it was, but as Pepe and Massimo neared the house, Pepe felt his legs almost give out. It was Alessandro.

Alessandro looked up as Pepe and Massimo approached. He stood as Pepe stepped onto the porch.

"*Come mai?* What's going on?" Pepe asked.

"*Posso?* May I?" Alessandro said as he leaned toward Pepe and gave him kisses on both cheeks.

"We'll leave you two," Zeno suggested as he stood and took hold of Patrick's hand, lifting him off his chair. They led Massimo inside.

"I'm surprised to see you," Pepe said. "But I'm glad you are here."

"I'm sorry for my silence."

"I'm sure things are complicated."

"They are, but I hope the news I have is encouraging."

Pepe's eyes widened. He stood. "Let's go to my place and talk."

They walked inside Pepe's house. "Make yourself at home. Open some wine and take out some cheese from the fridge. I need to clean up."

Pepe went outside and showered. He put on a fresh pair of shorts and a tee shirt and returned to the living room where Alessandro was sitting on the sofa, sipping wine.

Pepe sliced a sizeable chunk of cheese from a platter on the coffee table and plopped it in his mouth. He was starving. He poured himself a glass of wine and said, "Cheers. How are you doing?"

"Fine. Better."

"I didn't expect you."

"I know. I should have let you know I was coming. I guess I wanted to surprise you."

"It's a pleasant one."

"And how are you?" Alessandro asked Pepe.

"Okay. Not great, but okay."

"I'm sorry."

"It's fine. There are a lot of things to keep me busy this time of the year."

"Well, I'll get right to the point. I think I have rectified things. I told Giada that once the baby is born, I want to finalize the divorce and grant her full custody."

Stunned, Pepe was at a loss for words. After gathering his wits, he said, "Wow! I didn't see that coming. How did she react?"

"She has agreed. It would seem that one of her affairs has turned serious, and she wants to start a family with the guy."

"How does that make you feel?"

"I'm ambivalent. I'm glad there will be a definitive break, but I have mixed feelings about giving up the chance to have a son."

"So, the baby is a boy?"

Alessandro nodded.

"Is Giada living with this guy?"

"It would seem so."

"So, what's next for you?"

"That's why I'm here. I feel like I really messed things up between us. If there are any residual feelings, I would love to see if we could start over."

"Residual feelings?" Pepe exclaimed animatedly.

Alessandro grew alarmed.

Then Pepe said, "I think about you all the time."

Alessandro began to weep. He had hoped Pepe still had feelings for him, but he feared the worst. Pepe's declaration was a profound relief.

Pepe slid toward him and placed his arm around Alessandro's shoulder. "I'm proud of you. What a brave and difficult decision."

"I feel like I'm falling off a cliff. Everything is sliding out from under my feet – my marriage, my hopes for a family, and my career."

"Your career?" Pepe asked with concern.

"I haven't been able to focus. I've lost momentum at work."

"Hold it. Let's start over. Your marriage hasn't failed. You have both come to a greater appreciation for who you are, and you have made responsible decisions – decisions that are good for Giada and good for you. Second, unless you're changing teams again, there is still hope for a family."

"You think so?"

"Yes. But back to your litany of failures. Your career isn't over, either. You went through a rough patch, but you can rebuild. You're smart and personable and have good connections. By the way, are you hungry? I'm starving."

"I haven't had much of an appetite, worrying about things."

"What about some scallopine with marsala sauce?

"And some of your roasted potatoes?"

Pepe smiled and nodded. He reached into a drawer and pulled out a knife. "Can you cut up the potatoes? Small thin slices?"

Alessandro nodded obediently.

Pepe took out some veal and set them on a cutting board. He pounded them thin. A half-hour later, the potatoes were nice and crispy and the veal was simmering in a velvety marsala sauce. They prepared plates and sat at the table.

"Thanks for your understanding," Alessandro began.

"Thanks for your courage and persistence. I'm glad you are here."

"You don't mind?"

"I'm going to put you to work tomorrow. The *vendemmia* is in full swing."

"My timing is off."

"It's perfect."

"What's new with you?"

"Nothing."

Alessandro was dying to ask if Pepe had been seeing anyone. He'd have to be circumspect. "Any new paintings?" he asked, hoping to circle back to his real question at some point.

"I haven't had time or the motivation."

Alessandro felt a pit in his stomach. He realized Pepe had been hurting since Milan. "How are the grapes this year?" he asked, hoping to find a more upbeat topic of conversation.

"Good," Pepe said without elaboration. He felt a deep ambivalence and was at a loss for words. He could feel his body come to life. He craved the man in front of him, and that bothered him. Just a few hours earlier, he was angry and disappointed. Now he wanted to leap onto him and consume him.

Alessandro had said all the right things, but Pepe worried things could unravel quickly. Giada might grow disenchanted with her boyfriend and have second thoughts or complications. How would Alessandro react, then?

Despite his reticence, Pepe reached his hand over and stroked Alessandro's thigh. "You look different," he said softly.

Alessandro gave him a quizzical look.

"You've let your hair grow out. And you're tan from the summer. There's something else, too, but I can't quite put my finger on it."

"You look the same. Handsome as ever," Alessandro said, reaching for Pepe's hand. Pepe squeezed it but let go.

"Your eyes. That's it," Pepe suggested. "They are more intense, pensive, inquisitive."

"I'm hoping we might start over."

Pepe didn't say anything. He stood and reached for Alessandro's hand, lifting him up and leading him into the bedroom. It was obvious he wanted to start over.

Pepe sat on the edge of the bed with Alessandro and leaned forward, unbuttoning Alessandro's shirt and running his warm hands over Alessandro's chest. He pushed Alessandro back and straddled him, running his lips along the side of his pecs. Alessandro moaned.

Alessandro reached his hands around Pepe's waist and squeezed his firm buttocks. He could feel Pepe's growing erection press against his own. Pepe unzipped his shorts and slid them down his legs. His cock breached the confines of his undershorts and as he leaned back over Alessandro, it rested heavily on Alessandro's abdomen.

The sensation of Pepe's thick cock against his skin sent tremors through Alessandro's body. He reached under Pepe and skillfully pressed his own jeans and undershorts down his legs so that his sex sprung forth and their shafts grazed each other.

Pepe nuzzled his nose into Alessandro's neck and then whispered softly into his ear, "I've missed you so much."

Alessandro took the back of Pepe's head, tracing his fingers through the playful tufts of his hair, and pulled him close. He surrounded Pepe's lips with his own. Pepe opened his mouth and felt the warm moistness of their shared breath. Alessandro wrapped his arms and legs around Pepe and savored the melting of the demarcation between them. He felt Pepe's heart beat against his own.

Pepe wanted to thrust himself inside Alessandro, but knew that unnerved him. Alessandro felt Pepe's hardness searching ardently between his legs. He took a deep breath and spread them.

Surprised by Alessandro's move, Pepe murmured, "Are you okay?"

Alessandro didn't answer, but he pulled Pepe's body more tightly onto his. As they held each other tightly, their bodies perspired, their muscles tightened, and their pulses raced. Pepe felt the end of his cock slide against the inside of Alessandro's legs. He pressed deeper, and Alessandro squeezed his legs around him.

Pepe reached over to the bedside table and opened a drawer, pulling out a condom and some lube. He opened the package and slipped it on. He squeezed some lube onto his fingers and got his partner ready.

Alessandro reached down and took hold of Pepe's sex and guided it toward himself. Pepe contracted his buttocks and stretched toward and into Alessandro. Alessandro winced as he felt Pepe enter him. He took another deep breath and relaxed. Pepe felt Alessandro's warmth envelop him.

While plunged deep inside Alessandro, Pepe leaned up. He took Alessandro's legs and slid them over his shoulders. He thrust himself back and forth inside Alessandro. Alessandro reached for his own erection and ran his hand up and down the shaft.

Pepe gazed down at the handsome man beneath him. His eyes were ravenous yet tender.

Alessandro's breathing increased as he felt the end of his sex throb. He felt the solidity of Pepe's body filling the empty contours of his heart. He rode the arousal of their bodies - Pepe's thrusts inside him and the increased hardness of his own sex in his hand.

Pepe felt a last-minute twitch of anxiety course through his chest. He knew he was about to let go, about to let his heart pine for another, without reserve, all in.

Alessandro peered at the man towering over him, whose eyes were closed and face filled with delight. He hoped Pepe's remaining reticence might melt in their passion. Suddenly, he felt Pepe come – his cock vibrating powerfully inside him. He watched as Pepe arched his back, and his body twisted with pleasure.

Alessandro feared he might not come as Pepe's body relaxed. Remaining inside Alessandro, Pepe spit into his hand and took Alessandro's cock. He nimbly ran his fingers up and down the shaft. With each stroke, he squeezed the end of Alessandro's sex. "You are so fucking handsome," Pepe exclaimed as he held his lover and watched him travel to another dimension. Soon, Alessandro exploded in Pepe's hand, his body shuddering powerfully.

Pepe pulled himself out of Alessandro and collapsed onto his chest. Alessandro put his arm over Pepe's back, and they remained still, each realizing they had finally let go. It wasn't long before both fell into a deep and peaceful sleep.

16

Chapter Sixteen – Tangled Affections

A few days later, the *vendemmia* was over. Pepe and Alberto worked closely together to oversee the complicated and delicate fermentation process. Pepe had convinced Alessandro to stay with him for the foreseeable future. Zeno, Patrick, and Massimo were getting ready to return to Boston.

Alessandro wandered up to Zeno's and Patrick's house and knocked on the kitchen door.

"*Avanti,*" Zeno said, giving Alessandro an embrace as he walked in. "Coffee?" Zeno offered.

"That would be nice."

Patrick came in from the bedroom and said, "*Ciao,* Alessandro. How are you doing?"

"Good. Busy."

"Accounts all good?" Patrick followed up.

"Yes. We are back on track."

"And you can work from here?" Zeno inquired.

"Pepe's got me all set up in his studio."

"Do you guys want to come over for dinner tonight?" Zeno added.

"Actually, that's why I'm here. We wanted to invite you over. I got some nice pork chops at the market and was thinking about grilling them. Perhaps around six-thirty for appetizers?"

Zeno and Patrick glanced at each other and nodded. "Sure," Patrick said.

"Great. We'll see you later."

Later that evening, Pepe cleaned up from work and set out cheese, prosciutto, and olives on a platter. Patrick, Zeno, and Massimo arrived. Pepe offered them drinks, while Alessandro seasoned the chops and prepared some sauce for a pasta first course.

"I see Alessandro likes to cook, too," Patrick said as he lifted his glass to Pepe's and they took seats in the living room. Pepe sat next to Patrick on the sofa. Zeno took one of the large chairs and Massimo sat on the floor, watching a movie on his tablet.

"Are you guys ready to head to Boston?" Pepe asked.

"There's still a lot to do – closing up the house, packing, taking care of loose ends," Patrick replied.

"I can close up the house for you, and I can drive you to the airport," Pepe offered.

Patrick placed his hand on Pepe's thigh and said, "You're so generous. Thanks."

Alessandro came into the room and joined them. He squeezed in next to Pepe and placed his arm around his shoulder. He noticed Patrick's hand on Pepe's thigh. Pepe replied to Patrick's comment, saying, "I'm going to miss you guys."

"We'll miss you, too," Zeno said. "It's not the same when we are all separated."

"When will you be back?"

Zeno and Patrick glanced at each other. Patrick said, "We may come back around Thanksgiving, at the end of November. Certainly, we will be here for Christmas."

Pepe smiled contently.

Patrick reached toward the platter on the coffee table, continuing to brace himself with his hand on Pepe's leg. With Alessandro pressed in on one side, Pepe found more room leaning into Patrick. He breathed in the subtle fragrance of Patrick's cologne and felt the heat of his body. Alessandro played with the back of Pepe's hair, but Pepe could only focus on the occasional peeks of Patrick's chest as the front of his shirt opened slightly with each move.

Zeno stood and walked over to Massimo to check on him. Alessandro could feel Pepe pivoting toward Patrick. Alessandro got up and retreated to the kitchen.

A short while later, Alessandro called everyone to the kitchen table for dinner.

"Alessandro, this smells amazing," Zeno said as he gazed at the platter filled with chops that had been perfectly caramelized on the grill. Beside them was a bowl filled with rigatoni covered in a roasted eggplant sauce. "And I see you're acclimating to southern recipes!"

"I have a good teacher," he said, pulling Pepe toward him and giving him a kiss on his cheek.

Everyone took a seat and helped themselves.

"Delicious," Zeno said as he took a bite of the pasta.

Pepe reached over and put his hand on the top of Zeno's and said, "Alessandro has a lot of hidden talents."

Patrick raised a brow, Alessandro blushed, and Zeno took Pepe's hand and squeezed it. "Lucky for you," he said.

"Any trips planned?" Pepe asked.

Excitedly, Zeno placed his hand on Pepe's leg and said, "Patrick surprised us with a trip to Montreal. We will go in October, when the foliage is in full color."

Alessandro noticed Zeno's spontaneous affection toward Pepe, and Pepe's apparent delight at Zeno's touch. As the evening continued, Alessandro grew increasingly alarmed at the affection and intimacy between Zeno, Patrick, and Pepe. He was jealous, and he felt excluded.

Zeno, Patrick, and Massimo retired to their home after coffee and dessert. Alessandro and Pepe cleaned dishes. "Nice evening," Pepe said, giving Alessandro a rub on his shoulder and a kiss on his cheek. "Thanks for everything you did to make it a special evening. I'm glad we are all close."

Alessandro didn't respond. He dried some plates and placed them on the shelf.

"I'm going to miss them," Pepe added. "It's quiet when they are gone."

Alessandro felt the sting of Pepe's remark, fearing he wouldn't be enough for him. He tidied up the table, wrapped leftovers in foil, and followed Pepe into the bedroom.

Pepe shed his clothes, used the bathroom, and came back into the bedroom, sliding under the blankets. Alessandro did the same, turning away from Pepe in bed and hugged his pillows.

"*Buonanotte, tesoro,*" Pepe whispered.

Alessandro didn't respond. In fact, he began to weep.

Pepe sensed something was amiss and turned toward him. "*Che c'e?* What's wrong?"

Alessandro couldn't respond at first. Between sobs, he tried to formulate his thoughts. "I appreciate the relationship you and Zeno and Patrick have, but I guess I feel excluded."

"Oh, dear, no! You are not excluded. I'm so happy you are here, and I am so happy we are back together."

"But you are so affectionate with Zeno and Patrick. I feel like I'm hanging out on the periphery."

"No, no, no. You mean everything to me." He ran his hand over Alessandro's chest and along his side.

"Do you miss sex with Patrick and Zeno?" Alessandro asked point blank.

Pepe blushed. He hesitated and said, "I do sometimes. But our experiment didn't work. I need my own relationship."

"But it seems like you haven't moved on."

"We're family and neighbors. It's complicated."

"What if we lived in Milan, next door to Giada and her baby? How would you feel?" Alessandro said.

"That's different."

"How?"

"Giada doesn't respect you, your orientation, or your relationships. Zeno and Patrick love you and are happy for us."

"Do they?"

"Yes. I assure you. They know there are boundaries as well."

"I don't pick up on that. Everyone is quite affectionate with each other."

"We're Italian and family. That's it," Pepe tried to convince Alessandro. In fact, he was trying to convince himself that there were no lingering entanglements.

Alessandro buried his head in the soft pillows, giving them a tight squeeze. Pepe reached over and said, "Ale, I know how you must feel. I felt it when I was with Patrick and Zeno – an interloper, an appendage. You are not. I love you so much, and I want to make a family and a home with you. Never doubt that."

"I'm sorry. Maybe I overreacted."

"I'm glad you are honest with me. I need to know what you are thinking and feeling. Together, we can make this work." Pepe pulled Alessandro toward him and gave him a kiss. "Is it okay if I call you Ale?"

"No one has since I was a child. I like it."

"Good night, dear," Pepe said tenderly. He nuzzled himself against the back of Alessandro. They both fell quickly asleep.

17

Chapter Seventeen – Stefano

Toward the end of November, everyone gathered at Pepe's house for a visit from the foster care agency. Zeno, Patrick, and Massimo were back for a Thanksgiving visit.

"Is everything in place?" Pepe asked frantically, as he took a walk through the house.

"It's perfect," Alessandro said.

Patrick rubbed his hand over Pepe's shoulder and added, "Relax. Just be yourself."

Zeno nodded to Pepe and smiled.

"Son, I'm proud of you. You will make an incredible parent," Alberto said, giving his son a warm embrace. Maria squeezed his hand.

A car drove up, and a woman got out and walked to the door. Pepe opened the door for her. "You must be Priscilla."

"Yes. And you are Pepe?"

Pepe nodded, shook her hand, and welcomed her into the living room.

"Here's my family. My father and mother, Alberto and Maria."

"*Piacere*," they all said in unison.

"This is my cousin, Patrick, and his partner, Zeno."

Priscilla gave them a scrutinizing look and shook their hands. "And you have a son, right?"

"Yes. Massimo. He's with Zeno's parents."

Pepe then interjected, "And this is Alessandro. Part of the family."

"*Piacere*," Alessandro said, giving Priscilla a warm handshake.

"Where would you like me to sit?" Priscilla asked.

Pepe gestured for her to take a seat, and everyone else took their places.

"Well, let's get started," Priscilla began. "I've reviewed your application. I have to admit, this is an unusual situation."

Alarmed, Alberto asked, "How so?"

"Your history. I see you were adopted, Pepe."

He nodded.

"And I see that Patrick and Zeno adopted Massimo through the foster care system that replaced the institute."

Zeno and Patrick nodded.

"So your family has a history of creating nurturing homes for foster children. And you understand what is involved – firsthand."

Everyone smiled and relaxed.

"Your extended family network impressed my colleagues. Ordinarily, we don't like to place children with single parents. The laws have only recently changed to allow them. But we sense that if we place a child here, he or she will have a constellation of people co-parenting – grandparents, parents, cousins, aunts, and uncles. Can you speak to that, Pepe?"

Pepe cleared his throat. "Maria and Alberto have been incredible parents over the years. Not only did they welcome me into their home, Alberto made me an integral part of the family business."

"And that is winemaking, right?"

Everyone nodded.

"Alberto's two sisters have welcomed me and always treated me as their biological nephew. Ultimately, I would like to welcome a foster child into this loving family, just as everyone welcomed me."

Priscilla nodded.

"Zeno and Patrick, I don't know how you managed to circumvent the rules, but you convinced my former colleagues to place Massimo in your care. I see from the application that he is excelling in school and shows all evidence of being a well-adjusted young man," she said.

Alberto interjected, "Yes. Massimo has thrived here. One of the things that has impressed me over the years is how Pepe has taken Massimo under his wings. It is almost as if Massimo has a third parent."

Zeno and Patrick nodded and smiled.

"I'm convinced Pepe has the skill and the abilities to be an extraordinary father. And he won't be alone. All of us are here to support him."

Priscilla peered over at Alessandro and wondered who he was in the family. Since Zeno and Patrick were a gay couple, she wondered if Pepe and Alessandro were, too. As a closeted lesbian, she had no issue with Alessandro and Pepe adopting, but she had to be careful in what she documented.

"I see you have the financial resources to take care of a child."

Pepe nodded. "I have a secure position, salary, title to my home, and savings."

"That's all good," she noted.

"And if the foster situation worked out, would you be prepared to adopt?"

Pepe smiled and nodded yes.

"Would you be willing to welcome a child with disabilities?"

Pepe gave her a concerned look. "What kind?"

"I don't want to get into the details, but there's a possibility of placing a baby who was born prematurely. Physically, he will catch up. There is always a risk that there will be developmental disabilities – you know, psychological ones."

Pepe glanced across the room at Alessandro. Priscilla noticed. She waited for Pepe's response.

"We all have our challenges. A loving family is a powerful antidote," Pepe said.

Priscilla nodded pensively. She had already discovered Pepe's file in the archives and knew of the abuse he suffered in the orphanage. Pepe's response was thoughtful and reassured her of his compassion and the resources he could bring to a troubled child.

She asked more questions and took a tour of the house. Pepe made coffee for everyone and served them a piece of the ricotta pie he made earlier.

Priscilla looked at her watch and said, "Well, I should get back to Salerno. I will confer with my colleagues and be back in touch. It's been a pleasure. You have a wonderful family."

Alberto and Maria shook her hand and thanked her. Zeno and Patrick did the same.

Priscilla shook Pepe's hand warmly. "Thanks for your interest in taking in a foster child."

"It would be a joy to give back what I received."

"I sense that in you."

She turned to Alessandro and added, "It was a delight to meet you. You have a wonderful family."

Alessandro blushed and said, "Thanks for your visit and your humanity." He sensed she had figured things out and was trying to convey her support.

A week later, Priscilla called.

"*Pronto*," Pepe answer.

"Mr. Benevento?"

"*Si*. Is this Priscilla?"

"Yes. I have good news. We are looking for a foster parent to care for the baby I mentioned during the interview. The single mother has several psychological issues and doesn't feel like she can take care of the baby. She wants to offer it up for adoption."

"So, would I be a foster parent or adopted parent?"

"First, you would take the child as a foster parent. If all goes well, we can then process paperwork for the adoption, as long as the mother continues to relinquish her rights."

"Have doctors examined the baby?"

"Yes. His lungs and other organs are underdeveloped, but he seems otherwise healthy and is catching up to where he should be."

"And psychological issues?"

"Those won't be known for some time. It's possible the baby inherited some genetic predispositions or that other issues that will surface. These won't be known for years. Are you having second thoughts?"

"No. As a young boy, I was passed up for adoption multiple times. It's my chance to make sure someone else doesn't suffer the same."

Priscilla, choked with emotion, had a difficult time finding her voice. Finally, she said, "I'm glad to hear that."

"When can we come to pick him up?"

Priscilla noticed Pepe had used the term 'we' instead of 'I.'

"Can you come at the end of the week? Make sure you have a car seat and bring someone to help you."

"We'll see you later."

"Ciao," Priscilla concluded and hung up.

At the end of the week, Alessandro and Pepe drove to Salerno.

"You don't think it's a problem that I will be with you?" Alessandro inquired as they snaked their way along the coastal road.

"Priscilla said to bring someone. I don't think she will suspect anything."

"I wonder if she already has. She looked at me oddly during the interview."

"Well, if she had any problems, they haven't gotten in the way."

"But you are on probation until the adoption."

"Relax. We're fine. Just act like you know what you are doing, and no one will raise a brow."

"Hmm. I'm not sure."

They drove up to the agency and walked into Priscilla's office. She didn't seem surprised to see Alessandro, and welcomed them both warmly. She processed paperwork and soon a social worker drove up and brought the baby into the office. He wiggled inside the tight blanket wrapped around him.

Pepe stood and peered into the baby's eyes. He knew right away who he was.

"Do you have a name in mind?" Priscilla asked.

"Stefano. Stefano Benevento."

"Ancestor or relative of yours?"

"It's a long story. A complicated one that involved an adoption as well."

Priscilla recorded the name. The social worker handed Stefano to Pepe. Pepe began to weep. Alessandro's eyes teared up as well. "He's so beautiful," Pepe said.

"You're going to be a good father," she said confidently. "Do you have a car seat? Diapers? Milk? Other provisions?"

"Yes. My family has been incredible. We all pulled things together quickly. Stefano will have a good home and a loving family."

"I can see that," Priscilla said. "*Buona fortuna*. Let me know if you need anything."

Pepe and Alessandro put Stefano in the car seat and carefully drove home. When they pulled up to Pepe's house, everyone ran to greet the new family member — Maria, Alberto, Zeno, Patrick, and Massimo.

Confidently, Pepe carried Stefano into the house. Stefano seemed intrigued by the people surrounding him and smiled. Then he let out a cry.

"I think he's hungry," Maria said. "I'll warm some formula."

Massimo followed Maria into the kitchen and watched. He was eager to learn how to take care of his new cousin.

"And you named him Stefano?" Zeno asked, his eyes red with emotion.

"Look at him. Look at his eyes. They are the same."

"It's not possible," Zeno added.

Patrick studied him and said, "There is a resemblance. It's uncanny. You don't think there's a genetic link somewhere?"

"Who knows?" Pepe replied. "The important thing is that we are continuing the legacy of creating a home for someone who didn't have one. It's as if Stefano is looking down upon us."

"Or perhaps looking at us," Alberto noted, as Stefano looked up.

Maria returned from the kitchen and gave Pepe the bottle of milk. Pepe held Stefano and fed him. When Stefano grew tired, Pepe put him in the crib they had set up in Pepe's studio.

Pepe invited everyone to gather in the living room, where he served appetizers and drinks.

"Congratulations," Alberto proposed in a toast. "To the new father amongst us."

"To the new fathers amongst us," Maria interjected, nodding toward Alessandro. She wanted to make sure everyone knew Pepe and Alessandro were together and embarking on this adventure as a couple.

"*Salute!*" everyone said.

"To Stefano!" they added.

18

Chapter Eighteen – Rival

A month later, Pepe and Alessandro sat pensively on the sofa. Stefano was asleep.

"So, what did you tell her?" Pepe asked after learning Alessandro and Giada had just finished a contentious phone conversation.

"I told her she had to work this out herself. I've moved on."

"What did she want you to do?"

"Her boyfriend, Pino, left her. She wants us to get back together."

"You're kidding."

Alessandro shook his head no.

"Is she joking?"

"Unfortunately, she's serious. She's now saying the baby is definitely mine and that I have a responsibility."

"*Cazzate!* Bullshit!"

"I told her the same."

"And her reaction."

"She won't agree to the divorce."

"Until the baby is born?"

"Even after that."

"Can't you get around that?"

"It's a long, arduous battle. But at some point, yes. I'm sorry, Pepe. I hate to drag you into all of this."

"We're together. We'll fight it together."

Alessandro sighed.

"What does she want?"

"For me to come back to Milan and be with her."

"And?"

"I told her that is not possible. I told her based on the last communication we had, I moved on. At that point, she had a boyfriend who planned to marry her and raise the baby."

"So, that fizzled?"

"Seemingly."

"She can't keep changing her mind."

"That's Giada."

"So, what are we going to do?"

"Nothing. I told her the discussion is over. I'll remain married until the baby is born, but after that, we will divorce, and I will relinquish any paternity claims or rights."

"But she's not going to go along with that."

"We'll have to fight her," Pepe said unconvincingly.

Pepe shook his head. He didn't have a good feeling. He worried Alessandro would cave or Giada would come up with ways to make his life uncomfortable.

Two weeks later, Pepe received a call from Priscilla.

"*Ciao*, Priscilla."

"*Ciao*, Pepe. How is Stefano?"

"Good, thanks. He's growing quickly and seems to be adapting well to his new surroundings and family. He's very interactive."

"I'm sure you all give him a lot of attention."

"We do. What can I do for you?" Pepe hoped Priscilla might have information about moving the foster parent status toward a legal adoption.

Priscilla cleared her throat. "There's been a development."

"What kind?"

"The agency got a call from someone in Milan. He's a lawyer and wanted to file a complaint."

"About what?'

Priscilla didn't respond at first. Then she said, "He believes we placed a baby with a gay couple. Your baby."

Pepe felt his legs begin to shake nervously. "Based on what evidence?"

"He didn't enumerate."

"Why would that be his concern?"

"I'm sorry. This is all very confidential, and I probably shouldn't be sharing it with you."

"Don't worry. I'll be discreet," Pepe assured her.

"He represents Alessandro's wife. She claims Alessandro abandoned her and his paternal responsibilities. He believes Alessandro is your partner and is raising Stefano with you."

"I don't know what to say," Pepe replied, concerned about being transparent with Priscilla.

"Don't worry. I knew about you and Alessandro from the start. It was obvious in the way you looked at each other and the way your family referred to him as family, but with no specific designation."

"And you placed Stefano with us, anyway?"

"I knew you would be the perfect family."

"We haven't broken any laws. Alessandro and Giada came to an agreement that because of Alessandro's orientation, they would separate. Giada became pregnant before things could be finalized.

She claims it could be his baby, but she had relations with several other men. Alessandro agreed to remain married until the baby was born, but that the divorce would be finalized then, and he would relinquish paternity rights."

"The problem is, if we knowingly placed a baby with a gay couple, we could get in trouble. At the moment, it is a foster placement. But when things come up for review, our hands will be tied."

"*Cazzo!*" Pepe said in anger. "What would that mean?"

"We'd have to take Stefano back."

"But that's unfair to him. After over a month with us, he's grown attachments. He's making incredible progress, and his developmental milestones are all on target."

"I know. It isn't fair. And I can't imagine how hard it would be on you."

"Is there anything that can be done?"

"I'm working on some creative solutions. It will take me some time, but I thought I would alert you."

"Thanks for letting me know. Is there anything we should do?"

"I wouldn't let Alessandro's wife know you know about this. I'm not supposed to have told you."

"When will we hear from you next?"

"Soon. Within a week."

"Thanks for your call."

"I'm sorry."

Pepe hung up and went into the study where Alessandro was working.

"*Tesoro,* we have a problem."

Pepe explained what Priscilla had disclosed. Alessandro sat dumbfounded, incredulous as to how far even Giada might go to get her way and ruin his life.

"I'm going to fly to Milan and confront her."

"She's not supposed to know that we know."

"I'm not going to sit back and let someone else destroy my family."

"I appreciate that, but maybe we should be prudent."

"Giada doesn't respond to prudence. She needs a cudgel."

"We don't want to antagonize her."

"I won't. But I have a back-up plan."

"What?"

"I didn't want to tell you. I hoped it wouldn't come to this."

"You're scaring me."

"When she had her hospital episode in August, I went to the house to get some items she needed. I took the opportunity to hide mini cameras around the house."

Pepe's eyes widened. "You didn't?"

"I did. I feared I had lost you, and I wanted to get even. I also hoped that perhaps I could rectify things if she was uncooperative."

"Do you have recordings?"

"Quite a few. Most are from early in the pregnancy."

"And?"

"I have enough to get her to shut up."

"Why haven't you used them yet?"

"She's vindictive. If I did, she would come after the things that are most important to me — you and Stefano."

"It's too late. The agency knows about us."

"Yes, but I think Priscilla is an ally," Alessandro said.

"I do, too. But her hands are tied."

"Not if the lawyer from Milan retracts his complaint."

"How would he do that?"

"He could say that after further investigation, he realizes he was mistaken. He could clarify that the person of concern, Alessandro

Frantoia, is actually in the employment of the Benevento family, and not romantically involved with anyone there."

"Do you think the agency would buy it?"

"Priscilla would. And she can assuage the concerns others might have."

"We have nothing more to lose and everything to gain."

"I'll start composing some emails with attached files. Can you take care of Stefano while I focus on this?"

"Gladly."

19

Chapter Nineteen – Skiing in the Alps

I n late January, everyone gathered in Courmayeur to ski.

"This is amazing, Alessandro," Zeno said, as he sat on the sofa, gazing out of the large window at the snow-capped peaks towering overhead.

"My parents were fortunate in getting this years ago. And there's a cozy fireplace just for you," Alessandro noted.

"I knew I could rely on you."

"Where did Patrick and Massimo go?"

"To rent skis."

Pepe walked into the living room with Stefano in arm. He was squirming. "Since he slept all the way here in the car, he's restless."

"He hasn't started crawling yet, has he?" Zeno inquired.

"No, but he's very active. I imagine he will start soon," Pepe noted.

"That's a good sign that developmentally he's on target," Zeno added.

Alessandro approached Pepe and stood behind him, gazing at Stefano. His heart was at peace and full of joy. He and Giada had just signed divorce papers in Milan. One of her new boyfriends was eager to claim paternity in exchange for the lifestyle she could extend to him, so a quick divorce and remarriage suited her. Alessandro presumed his trump card had motivated her, too. Alessandro could now relax and trust that his new family would be free from harassment or complications.

Zeno, Patrick, and Massimo flew up to meet Pepe, Stefano, and him for an impromptu and celebratory ski vacation.

Patrick and Massimo walked into the chalet. "Where do we put these?" he asked Alessandro as he juggled his and Massimo's skis, boots, helmets, and poles.

"There's a ski closet right inside the door."

"Ah. Here it is. Thanks."

"Did you get everything you needed?"

"They were very helpful. And look, it's snowing!"

Alessandro glanced out of the window. Big beautiful flakes were falling from the darkening ski.

"Do we need to go to the market?" Patrick asked.

Alessandro nodded no. "I have sauce in the freezer and plenty of wine."

"Breakfast?" Zeno pressed.

"We have coffee, croissants that I can defrost and cook, marmalade, and cereal. I can go to the corner market to get some cream and milk. We have everything we need for Stefano."

"I'll make a fire, and we can settle in for the evening," Alessandro said.

Later, they gathered around the dining table. Massimo was excited to go skiing and Patrick kept checking the ski map to chart their day.

"You two are so cute!" Alessandro observed.

"I can't believe we are going to ski in Europe," Patrick said excitedly.

"Do you miss Vermont? Boston?" Pepe asked.

"A little," Patrick said. "But I'm glad we made the decision to stay here in Italy. The back and forth was getting more and more difficult, and we didn't like being away from you all."

Pepe smiled. "I'm so glad we are all together." He made a point to take hold of Alessandro's hand to reassure him of where his heart and affections rested.

"So, everything is finalized with Giada?" Patrick asked.

Alessandro nodded. "We signed the papers yesterday."

"And with the agency in Salerno?" Patrick asked Alessandro and Pepe.

"We can't adopt as a gay couple, but the adoption papers have been processed for me. I am Stefano's legal parent," Pepe said with pride.

"I'm sure that wasn't easy," Zeno observed.

"Alessandro was able to exert pressure on Giada's family to retract the allegations they had secretly made to the agency. Priscilla was able to convince her colleagues that all was in order — that Pepe was bringing a son into a large extended family network that included Alessandro without identifying his role. And a follow-up visit to our home assured Priscilla and one of her colleagues that Stefano was flourishing and in a good place. Priscilla is on our side," Pepe concluded.

"I believe someday you will be able to co-adopt as a gay couple in Italy. Things are changing."

"They are," Alessandro said. "But slowly."

"I'm encouraged by our family," Pepe said. "They are not liberal city people, yet they have embraced us all."

"Speaking of which," Alessandro began. "What's happening with you and Nunzia?" he asked Patrick.

"When she found out we wanted to settle here full time, she shared her dream of opening a restaurant adjacent to the inn. An older couple was selling their retail shop. Nunzia has asked me to manage the new enterprise."

"That's a lot of work."

"Yes, but it allows me to work close to home. I might even try to steal a waiter from another restaurant," he said, raising a brow and looking at Zeno.

"Work for you?" Zeno exclaimed, furrowing his brow. "I don't think so."

Everyone chuckled. Pepe had already been thinking about how to create a side of Patrick's business that might include a small market with items such as local wine, honey, and other agricultural products.

"Massimo, are you ready to ski tomorrow?" Alessandro asked.

He nodded enthusiastically. "Will you come with me and dad and show us around?"

"With pleasure. I learned to ski here as a boy."

"Are you sure you don't want to ski?" Patrick asked Zeno.

"Certain. Pepe and I will hang here and watch Stefano."

"And the fireplace, right?" Patrick interjected.

Zeno smiled and glanced at Pepe.

"We'll go to the market and pick up things for dinner," Pepe noted.

Alessandro yawned and said, "Hey, guys. I'm getting tired. I think I'm going to go to bed. Feel free to stay up, watch TV, or whatever."

"I'll come with you," Pepe said. "I'll feed Stefano. Hopefully, he will fall asleep."

Zeno and Patrick looked at each other. Patrick said, "Well, Massimo. If we are going to ski tomorrow, we need to get our rest. Why don't you head to your room? Papa and I will head to ours."

Massimo didn't put up any resistance to the idea of going to bed. He was eager to go to sleep and wake up for a day on the slopes.

Pepe fed Stefano and put him in a small bed they had placed in their room. He used the bathroom and crawled into bed with Alessandro. They heard a few whimpers from Stefano, then he got quiet.

"Sounds like he's asleep," Alessandro said.

"Yes. Thank God!"

"Thanks for everything," Alessandro said, rubbing his hand over Pepe's chest.

"I can't believe it. You are free. We are together. We have a son!" Pepe murmured to him.

"Yes, it's a dream come true. And look who I'm sleeping with!"

Pepe pivoted toward Alessandro and ran his hand along Alessandro's side toward his waist. He felt the contours of Alessandro's buttocks, firm and round. He felt his sex firming up against him.

The last couple of weeks had been stressful, and neither had been relaxed enough to make love. Pepe felt confident about things, and he was ready to celebrate by staking his claim – consuming the luscious man nestled next to him.

He stroked Alessandro's increasingly erect shaft. Alessandro moaned and ran his hand between Pepe's legs and along his cock.

Pepe licked Alessandro's smooth, firm chest and breathed in his scent. He felt the warmth of his skin against his face and the hardness pressed between his legs. Alessandro wrapped his legs around

Pepe and pulled him close. He savored the solidity of Pepe's body on his — the security and intimacy it promised.

Both clung to each other, the heat of their bodies an antidote to the cold mountain air outside. Pepe kissed Alessandro's ear, then his neck, then his side. He continued down Alessandro's abdomen and then pivoted, taking Alessandro in his mouth.

Alessandro reached up and took Pepe's sex, stroking the supple and hot skin. Pepe let out a cry of delight and fell back onto the mattress. Alessandro leaned over and peered into Pepe's dark eyes.

"I want you inside me," Pepe whispered. It was an unprecedented declaration, and Alessandro's eyes widened.

"Are you sure?" Alessandro asked.

Pepe nodded. He spread his legs.

Alessandro ran a hand along the inside of Pepe's legs. Pepe moaned.

Incredulously, but excitedly, Alessandro reached into the bedside table and pulled out a condom, sliding it on his hard, erect sex. He pressed himself against Pepe, who was ready to let Alessandro in – fully and without hesitation. Alessandro spit on his fingers and wet Pepe's opening. He slid himself inside and felt the tight warmth surround his sex.

It was a new sensation for both, a union that promised trust, passion, and joy. Alessandro flexed his buttocks and thrust himself deeper and deeper. Love was no longer out of reach, unattainable, elusive. He held Pepe in his arms. His body was an extension of his own.

Pepe felt Alessandro's embrace and the power of his sex filling him. He was no longer ancillary – but rather a partner, a father, and a vital member of the Benevento family. There were no longer voids to fill, but plans to make and dreams to achieve.

With each thrust, Pepe celebrated the control Alessandro was taking of destiny and of their lives together. Pepe squeezed Alessandro inside him, the two of them taking turns assuring the other of their force and determination.

Pepe took hold of his own sex and slid his hand up and down it. In synch with Alessandro, he felt himself grow larger, firmer. He closed his eyes and rode the waves of pleasure course through his body. Suddenly, he felt Alessandro's sex erupt inside him – a gentle but potent cascade of vibrations that reverberated through his body. He felt his own sex quiver and then explode in his hand.

Alessandro collapsed on top of Pepe, his arms wrapped around Pepe's shoulders. They both waited for their breathing to calm and their hearts to return to normal.

"I love you so much," Alessandro said quietly in Pepe's ear.

"I've been waiting for you all my life. I'm so glad you are finally here. I love you, too."

The End (At least for now)

Author

Michael Hartwig is a Boston and Provincetown-based author of LGBTQ+ fiction. Hartwig is an accomplished professor of religion and ethics as well as an established artist. Hartwig grew up in Dallas but spread his wings early – living in Rome for five years, moving to New England later on, and then working in the area of educational travel to the Middle East and Europe.

His fiction weaves together his interest in LGBTQ studies, ethics, religion, art, languages, and travel. The books are set in international settings. They include rich descriptions and are peppered with the local language. Characters grapple not only with their own gender and sexuality but with prevailing paradigms of sexuality and family in the world around them. Hartwig has a facility for fast-paced plots that transport readers to other worlds. They are romantic and steamy as well as thoughtful and engaging. Hartwig imagines rich characters who are at crossroads in their lives. In many instances, these crossroads mirror cultural ones. There's plenty of sexual tension to keep readers on the edge of their seats, but the stories are enriched by broader considerations – historical, cultural, and philosophical.

Other Titles:
Crossing Borders
Old Vines
Entwined
Oliver and Henry
A Roman Spell
Love Unearthed
Our Roman Pasts
Don't Push Me
A Collision in Quebec
Man By the Pool
Transito Seville

For More Information visit: www.michaelhartwigauthor.com

www.ingramcontent.com/pod-product-compliance
Ingram Content Group UK Ltd.
Pitfield, Milton Keynes, MK11 3LW, UK
UKHW020915240625

6550UKWH00033B/430